BEYOND ABSOLUTION

KEIRON COSGRAVE

49
In
Indium Publishing
114.818

WOULD YOU MAKE A BARGAIN WITH
THE DEVIL?

www.keironcosgrave.net

Facebook: Keiron Cosgrave Author
Cover and Interior Design, Editor: Author
Proof reader: Kirsty Ford
Publisher: Indium Books
Fourth Edition - May 2021(P)

Reader's note: This novel has been written in British English.

We operate a policy of continuous improvement. Every effort is made to minimise errors, typos, issues of grammar, etc. Occasionally, despite our best efforts, errors creep through. Reader feedback is actively encouraged and appreciated via the contact form on the website.

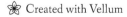 Created with Vellum

1

SATURDAY 18TH DECEMBER 1971, 11.00 P.M

Eleven-year-old Niall Daley glimpsed movement in his peripheral vision, beyond the bedroom door. A shadowy form dimmed the soft yellow light. Slipping beneath the blanket, he held his breath.

Two silent, dark minutes passed.

A latch clicked, hinges groaned, and a thickset man in a cassock appeared in the opening. Stepping in, the door swung closed behind him and darkness reclaimed the room.

Peeking above the blanket, Niall recognised Father Flynn O'Connell's face captured by moonlight. The air infused with whisky breath. O'Connell halted at the side of the bed.

Unseen in the darkness, Niall lay perfectly still and prayed.

Niall felt O'Connell's stubby, spidery fingers scuttle and stall on his thigh. Exhaling, he said: 'Father, please stop. It's sinful.'

'My child, shh!' O'Connell rasped. 'Stay still.' A hiccup captured under a clenched fist. 'Be quiet. This is God's will.' The rising hand of the wind rattled the window frames and peppered the glass with sand. O'Connell's mucous rasps amplified tenfold in the darkness. Captured by moonlight, the crucifix above the bed reflected in the mirror opposite.

Grasping the blanket, O'Connell dumped it on the floor and settled on the edge of the bed.

Frozen air swam over the Niall's face and the dark, paralysing hand of fear tightened around his throat. Leathery wanton fingers rampaged across his pale flesh.

'Father,' begged Niall, 'don't... It's too soon...'

O'Connell's fingers stalled, and he exhaled a sigh. Anger erupted in cold blue eyes. 'If I've told you once, I've told you a thousand times, quieten down. Otherwise, you're going to wake everyone. I don't want to hear another peep from you. Do you understand?'

A quarter minute passed in silence.

'Well, do you?'

'I'm sorry, Father,' Niall said, 'only...'

'Only nothing! Stay still. And for the love of God, relax. This won't take long.'

'I'm sorry,' Niall muttered.

'Don't be. We're in God's hands. Spin over onto your front.'

Niall gripped the mattress and rolled onto his front.

'Good boy.'

O'Connell's laboured breaths quickened. Time expanded and became eternal.

Ten minutes later, a spent O'Connell lifted from the bed, lowered his cassock, crossed to the basin and washed his hands and splashed cold water over his face. Returning bedside, he lowered into the armchair.

He spoke in a hushed voice, each syllable weighed and measured. 'Niall,' he said, reclaiming a hip flask from a cassock pocket. 'Tonight, I am the Lord's servant. We are both servants of the one true, almighty Lord.' O'Connell slugged whisky, spun the cap on, returned the flask to a pocket. 'The Lord knows this. Our one true Lord knows everything under the sun and stars. He knows you gave yourself tonight to repent your mortal sins. He loves you for it.'

O'Connell's voice ebbed to silence. He burped. Rising from the armchair, he spread his arms wide, burped again, and mumbled an apology to an unseen audience. Dizzy, losing his balance, he slumped against the wall beside the door. Rallying, he pushed from the wall and stood swaying over Niall and cast his arms wide once more. He stood as if he were addressing a Sunday congregation from the pulpit. 'We thank you, Lord, for bringing us together on this foulest of winter nights. Tonight, Lord, we are one in and through you. Our souls, bodies and minds, cleansed in your service...'

Another raucous burp, silence for a quarter minute. 'Now, let us pray...'

O'Connell ended the prayer in an incoherent slur.

'Amen.'

2

WEDNESDAY 31ST DECEMBER 2014, 8.00 A.M

James 'Jimmy' McNiff's mobile phone dinged. The *new message received* icon flashed. He stared at the handset. Sniffing, he stabbed a triangular piece of toast into his mouth and sucked butter from his fingers. Slurping tea, he scooped up the phone and studied the screen. The message was from old school friend, Niall Daley.

Not a little surprised, frowning, Jimmy gazed at the message. He had last seen Niall at a school reunion two years before. The intervening years dissolved in a haze of mind-numbing heavy metal, drink and drugs.

The message read:

```
check your email... call me ASAP... I've half
an hour free b4 work... it's very important!
concerns billy... our billy... cheers, con
                . . .
```

Jimmy tabbed to email, located Niall's message and jpeg attachment, selected it and pressed green. Sitting back, he finished the lukewarm tea. As the *opening* icon spiralled, glancing at the wall clock, he willed it to finish.

Fifteen seconds later, a blurred image – a newspaper cutting – filled the tiny screen. The image found focus, column inches, and a handwritten date scrawled above the headline. Jimmy expanded the image until it filled the screen.

30/12/2014

MASHAM FARMHAND FOUND HANGED

Retired army officer Jonathan Rainton discovered neighbour, Billy Searle, 52, dead at his home early yesterday morning. Police recovered a black karate belt from the scene. Mr Rainton said, 'I was due to collect a mini digger from Northallerton yesterday morning. I'm digging out an ornamental fishpond. Billy volunteered to help. That was typical of him. Getting no answer at the front door, I looked in through the lounge window. That's when I saw him. It was terrible. Billy was a likeable guy, a nice man and a good neighbour. He was always happy to lend a hand whenever you needed one. This comes as a great shock. He had everything to live for. Though Billy kept himself to himself, he had a close circle of friends. I can't say that I know much about his family. He once told me he'd a tough childhood. Said his parents sent him away to boarding school when

**he was ten. That he hated it. I do not know
what he meant by it. I didn't want to press him
about it. You don't, do you? Everyone who had
the pleasure of knowing Billy will miss him. My
heart goes out to the family.' Local GP Archie
Hamilton certified Mr Searle dead at the scene.
North Yorkshire Police confirm they are not
seeking anyone in connection with Mr Searle's
death.**

Jimmy's mind reeled. He lowered the volume on the radio and Chris Evans's shrill and annoyingly chirpy voice fell silent. He returned his gaze to his mobile. Re-read the message several times. Tabbing through the menu, he chose Niall Daley from contacts and pressed call.

'Jimmy. Thanks for calling back. Shit news,' Niall said, solemnly.

'I'll say. It's shocking. It isn't right. Billy would never commit suicide.'

'I know. I don't understand it either. It's true, though. Billy's dead. I had a brief conversation with his sister, Sharon, last night.'

'You did?'

'Yeah, do you remember Sharon, Jimmy? Lay back and think of England, Sharon?'

'How could I forget? She's difficult to forget, is Sharon.'

'The police picked her up and took her to the morgue late Monday night.'

'OK.'

'She identified the body. It's Billy, alright.'

'Christ. Awful,' Jimmy exclaimed. 'Why on earth would the daft sod kill himself?'

'Why do you think?'

Jimmy inhaled. 'I know, Con. But it was a long time ago. To my mind, whoever coined the phrase time heals, nailed it.'

'Oh, yeah?'

'Yeah, they did,' Jimmy said, pausing. 'At the reunion, he seemed happy with his lot. It's just such a massive shock. I can't believe we're having this conversation.'

'I'm hurting too. It's so sad.'

Jimmy cleared his throat. 'Was the poor bastard depressed? Was anything preying on his mind?'

'Not that I know of, no. It's strange. A couple of weeks ago, he called me out of the blue and invited me to York for the weekend to help him celebrate his birthday. The usual: beer, curry, and a club. You know the form. We planned to share on a room. Make a night of it. He sounded fine. I was looking forward to it,' Niall said.

'You two were always close.'

'We were. Back then, we were like brothers. The thing is, Jimmy – the thing I can't get my head around – is why he'd make plans for his birthday, and then top himself? It makes no sense.'

Silence.

'Jimmy, you there?'

'Yeah, I'm here. Sorry, I was thinking.'

'I thought I heard cogs turning.'

'Bugger off. What I was thinking was... Can suicide ever make sense? Does anyone really know what's going on inside someone's head?'

'I suppose not. You're right. It's surreal. Why on earth would he kill himself though, after all we've been through?'

'The police, Con, are they absolutely sure it was suicide?'

'I believe so. That's what they told Sharon. Why? You don't seriously believe he was murdered, do you?' Niall asked.

'That's not what I'm saying. But Billy committing suicide? I just can't see it. He wasn't the type. Billy was a survivor. We *all* are. We've had to be. We *survive*. That's what we do. You know that.'

'True enough,' Niall said. 'I'm sorry, I've got to go, otherwise I'm going to be late for work. Let's keep in touch. As soon as I know a date for the funeral, I'll give you a bell. We'll meet up, the three of us. Have ourselves a piss-up. Give Billy a good send-off. I've got Colm's mobile number somewhere. I'll give him a bell.'

'Best of British with that,' Jimmy said. 'Tosser never picks up when I call.'

After an awkward silence lasting several seconds, Jimmy said, 'Maybe, he doesn't recognise your number? I'll try him tonight. Let him know what's happened. In the meantime, take care of yourself. As soon as I know anything, I'll give you a bell. You OK with that?'

'I am, yeah. I'd appreciate it. Take care of yourself, Con. And thanks for letting me know. It can't have been easy.'

'It wasn't. Billy was a good person and friend. I'm sorry, but I've got to make a move. See you later, Jimmy.'

'Yeah, bye, Con.'

A spasm of pain speared through Jimmy's chest and he slumped into a chair, closed his eyes. A silent minute passed. A solitary tear coursed down his left cheek. Melancholy swallowed his heart. Opening his eyes, he glared at his reflection returned in the oven door glass.

'If that's how you want to play it, bastards, then so be it.'

THURSDAY 1ST JANUARY 2015, 8.30 A.M

Niall stepped outside into the brilliance of a sparkling winter morning. The low east sun warmed his face. Jewels of frost glistened from the concrete path and dusted the grass. He drew a deep breath, shuddered as the chill entered his lungs. Raising his face, he marvelled at the unblemished pastel blue sky. A chattering blackbird scuttled past, inches above the road, breaking him from his reverie.

As Niall closed the door, he heard the Yale click reassuringly into the frame. With a bounce in his step, he set off along the path for work. Swinging left, he quickened his pace.

Three cars lengths along the pavement, a smart-dressed, tanned, bald man in a camel coat, leaned against the flank of a white rental van, gaze directed at polished brogues, arms folded. A slip of white paper dangled from his right hand.

Unfolding his arms, he checked the time on his watch. Niall saw the watch was expensive: a Breitling, TAG, or similar. Gaze fixed on the pavement, Niall quickened his step. Parallel with the rear of the van, the man stepped out, blocking the pavement. Niall halted, expensive cologne filled his nostrils. He looked up.

'Morning,' Niall said, blanching.

Cold, dead eyes met Niall's. 'Is it?'

'Can I help you?'

'Directions,' the man barked, thrusting the paper at Niall. 'I need directions.'

Niall collected and studied the paper. 'I'll do my best.' Both sides were blank. 'Is this a wind-up, mate?'

With his question hanging in the air, Niall glimpsed a grey blur coming towards him and felt it spear him in the gut. A hand firm in the cleft of his back.

Niall yelped. 'What the hell?'

'Button it,' the man growled. 'Stay calm. Keep it buttoned. Alright?'

'Alright! Alright...'

The tanned man glanced around. Satisfied no one had noticed, he returned his gaze to Niall. 'This ain't no wind-up. I don't do humour, *mate*... Look at me. Pretend we're talking. Make it look natural. Try to make a run for it and I'll blow you away. What you're feeling is the business end of a gun. A Beretta. Silenced. One of my all-time favourites. Thing is, mate, I've got an itchy trigger finger. Turn around nice and slow. Climb into the van head first. Lay on your stomach. Don't, *repeat*, don't, even think about taking off, *mate*. Because if you do, I'll take great pleasure in scratching that itch.'

Reaching left, the man sprung the van's back doors, open. 'After you...'

Niall smirked. 'Piss off.'

'Get in!'

'You're joking... right?'

The tanned man looked away. A silent half minute passed. He returned his gaze to Niall. 'No, mate, I ain't. Do I look like I'm fucking joking?'

Niall felt the pressure release in his guts. Looked down and saw a silenced pistol. Felt it spear his gut again.

'I'm impatient. I'm going to ask you one last time. Get into the fucking van.'

Niall hesitated. The flight instinct took hold. The man, sensing it, shook his head.

'Not a good idea. Get in.'

Niall stepped left, scrambled inside, and lay face down on the bare metal floor.

'Arms back. Hands together. Fingers joined.'

Putting arms behind his back, Niall felt bands of ice-cold steel tighten around his wrists.

'Not a squeak. I hear anything, and you're a dead man. Got it? Just nod.'

Niall nodded.

'Good. You and I, we're going on a trip.'

The van's back doors clattered closed. Locks ground into place. All trace of daylight expunged from the freezing metal cell.

FRIDAY 2ND JANUARY 2015, 11.00 A.M

James 'Jimmy' McNiff walked into the main police station at Whitby with an acid feeling of resolve burning in his gut. Crossing to the reception desk, he cleared his throat and a uniformed officer with three stripes on his lapel, dragged his gaze from the computer screen. Jimmy put down a sealed envelope and slid it across the smooth Formica. Removing his hand, he stepped back. The Desk Sergeant – a ruddy-faced man in mid-to-late fifties – lowered his spectacles and studied the envelope with weary indifference.

His gaze lifted to Jimmy. 'Can I help you, sir?'

'I hope so, I'd like to speak to a detective. Someone senior. Name's James McNiff. Friends call me Jimmy.'

'What, may I ask, would you like to speak to a senior detective about, Mr McNiff?'

'Serious crimes, against defenceless young boys. It's all there, in writing, inside the envelope. I've prepared a statement. I've signed a copy.'

The Desk Sergeant's eyes narrowed, lips pursed. 'I see. What do you mean by serious crimes, sir? As I'm sure you'll appreciate, we get all sorts coming in here alleging all manner of things.'

Jimmy leaned forward. 'Abuse,' he whispered, eyes flaring, 'of the sexual kind.'

The Desk Sergeant sat back, folded his arms across his chest, heaved a sigh. 'I'm sorry, sir, only I'm going to need more than that. Do you mind if I read this statement of yours? This *statement of fact.*' The Sergeant's voice rose on the final three words.

Jimmy stepped back, shoulders shrugging, arms cast wide. 'Fine. Go ahead. That's why I'm here. Do what you have to do.'

The Desk Sergeant opened the envelope with a pencil, took out and unfolded an A4 sized sheet of paper and pressed it flat against the desk. Leaning forward, he set his elbows on the counter, returned his spectacles along his nose and read Jimmy's statement in silence.

STATEMENT OF FACT

Prepared by James Anthony McNiff of 144 Staithes Road, Sandsend, Nr. Whitby, North Yorkshire, on 1st January 2015.

This statement contains facts. Everything stated is true. It relates to my time as a boarder at St Aubert's Boarding School for Boys, Robin Hood's Bay from 1970 to 1976 (aged 10 to 16).

Myself and several other boys suffered regular physical, mental and sexual abuse at the hands of two priests and one nun.

We continue to be victims.

My abusers were,

Father Flynn O'Connell. He inflicted anal intercourse, made me perform oral sex and forced mutual masturbation. When I resisted, I suffered canings and beatings. I experienced daily psychological abuse. He also made me watch violent pornographic material.

Father Bryan Murphy. He facilitated and concealed O'Connell's sexual abuse and, occasionally, took part. He abused me in the same ways as O'Connell.

Sister Mary O'Toole. She facilitated and concealed sexual abuse by both priests and inflicted severe canings to myself, and others.

I believe Father Flynn O'Connell lives at Minster Mews Retirement Home in York, North Yorkshire.

I am unaware of Father Bryan Murphy's whereabouts. I last saw him in late September 1975. I recall he disappeared from St Aubert's and no one knew why. One day he was there, the next day he was gone. It was a mystery. There were rumours going around.

I heard a rumour five years ago that Sister Mary O'Toole retired to a convent in Cork, Republic of Ireland.

The other victims are my old school friends:

Billy Searle (Billy committed suicide (ref. Article in the Yorkshire Post, dated 30/12/2014),

Niall Daley,

Colm Walsh.

I have contact details for both Niall and Colm. I remain in regular contact with Niall.

I'd like to discuss another serious matter with a Senior Detective, at the earliest possible time.

Those named ought to be brought to justice. They inflicted terrible crimes against defenceless children. They abused me and many others. Our teachers abused the trust placed in them by the school and parents. To this day, my parents know nothing of the abuse I suffered during my time at St Aubert's.

These terrible events happened. The actions of our abusers have resulted in severe mental trauma. Physical scars disappear with time. Mental scars can never heal.

They have destroyed lives. Mine included. Their terrible legacy lives on in those they abused. It lives today, every day, and forever. None of us achieved our potential in life. Our failures are a direct consequence of the abuse we suffered at their hands.

I demand JUSTICE. WE demand JUSTICE.

I expect a thorough, competent and professional investigation. I wish to see the perpetrators imprisoned for the balance of their natural lives. Myself and the other victims ought to receive significant financial compensation. However, this isn't about the money.

Twenty years have passed, yet the pain

`continues. The pain will stay with me until my`
`dying day.`
`    Sincerely,`
`    James Anthony McNiff`
`    Sandsend, Whitby, January 2015.`

The Desk Sergeant straightened, folded, and returned the paper to the envelope. Joining his arms across his chest, he pinched his nostrils together, brow creased in thought.

'Sir, these are serious allegations. Before I take this any further, I need your personal assurance that everything you allege is, in fact, true. It is my duty to remind you, wasting police time is a very serious offence. Making malicious allegations can attract a custodial sentence.'

Jimmy nodded. 'As God is my judge, every allegation is true. I only wish this wasn't the case. Sergeant, those bastards – the priests and nuns – have ruined my life.'

'I see,' the Desk Sergeant said, stepping around the counter, a frown puckering his forehead. 'And, you're absolutely sure you want to move forward with these allegations? I have to ask.'

'Yes. That's the reason I'm here.'

The Desk Sergeant's frown evaporated. 'I hope you understand, sir, I have to ask such questions. Resources being what they are nowadays, time wasters are the bane of my life. A fundamental part of my job is sorting the wheat from the chaff, so to speak.'

Jimmy nodded. 'I understand.'

The Desk Sergeant nodded to the row of grey plastic chairs along the back wall.

'Take a seat, sir. I need to make a phone call. Can I get you a hot drink while you're waiting?'

'I'm OK, thanks,' Jimmy replied, taking a seat. 'All I need is a senior detective. We'll take it from there.'

'I'm sure you will, sir. I'm sure you will...' the Desk Sergeant said, returning behind the counter.

DS David Watts of North Yorkshire Police Major Crimes Unit picked up the Desk Sergeant's call on the third ring.

5

MONDAY 9TH JUNE 1975, 6.30 P.M

Evelyn and Colm ran along the footpath, guided by diagonal shafts of golden sunlight blasting through the canopy. Early June, and already it felt like high summer. Ahead, a trillion flies danced above tall grasses swaying gently in the heat haze of the late afternoon. The torpid air flavoured with wild garlic, fir and bramble.

'I reckon we've come far enough,' Evelyn gasped in the softest of Irish brogues. 'I can't go on... Honest, I can't...'

Hearing her voice, Colm's heart overflowed with joy.

Reaching up, Evelyn spun open two blouse buttons and revealed the voluptuous curves of her freckled, milk-white cleavage, glistening with sweat. Sat amongst the buttercups, tall grass and flies, she threw out her legs and lay back.

Colm, looming over Evelyn, caressed fledging breasts with electric blue eyes and savoured pert nipples straining against the thinnest of white cotton blouses. Those same eyes wandered towards the delicate curve of plump hips. Standing there, he smelt her musk and felt an urgent hardening between his legs. He reached down, adjusted his groin and gazed up at the perfect cerulean sky. Gathered breath, he admonished himself for having impure thoughts. He untied his jumper around his waist and lay it on the ground.

'Sit on this. You'll get grass stains otherwise. They'll notice. You know what they're like.'

Evelyn, smiling, lifted and dragged Colm's jumper under her hips. Colm glimpsed his reflection in the brown pools of her eyes. His gaze devoured tantalising scarlet lips, milky skin and auburn hair.

'Why did you bring me here?' *She asked.* 'I hope you're not planning on taking advantage of a defenceless wee girl?'

A grinning Colm adjusted his groin. Evelyn, noticing his ardour, smouldered with desire.

'I'd never do that. I respect you. Anyway, you're a nun. It wouldn't be right.'

'I'm a novice, that's what I am. I won't become a nun for another two years. I make the final decision. The Church doesn't own me. I'm not a chattel.'

'Is that how it works?'

'Yes, it is. It's me and me alone, who'll decide whether I take my final vows. Till then, I'll do what I want, when I want. Sister Mary – spiteful old hag – can go hang.'

Evelyn spread the jumper across the grass, so Colm could sit close.

'Sit down, why don't you? I don't bite,' *she said, trying hard not to stare at his burgeoning groin.* 'Look at you, Colm Walsh, standing to attention all big and proper. Sit down, horny dog. You're embarrassing me.'

Colm's cheeks flushed deep crimson. 'I'm sorry,' *he said, sinking to the ground.*

They lay gazing at the sky without speaking. High in the canopy above them, a wood pigeon cooed and a song thrush chattered. In the distance, lambs bleated, and farm machinery droned.

Evelyn said, 'How far have we come?'

'Two; perhaps three miles. I'm not sure.'

'Far enough, then?'

Evelyn pushed up on an elbow, rolled onto him and sank against his chest. She brushed his lips with hers.

'Far enough for what?' Colm said, grinning, feeling Evelyn's breath hot against his skin.

'Far enough so no one can hear, silly. You're the world's biggest eejit, Colm Walsh. You really are.'

'Hear us doing what?' He said with a wry smile.

She tutted, giggled. 'Now I know you're taking the mickey!'

'Who, me?'

'Who else would I be referring to?' Evelyn said, lifting his t-shirt, stroking his stomach, fingers inching down.

Her fingers found him. They kissed long and hard. Releasing herself from his embrace, she took a firm grip on his manhood.

Eyes wide, he groaned.

'Don't be shy. We both know the reason we've come this far. It isn't to study the flora and fauna now, is it? Beautiful though it is. I've seen the way you look at me at morning mass. I've seen you undressing me with your eyes. You've brought me this far so you can have your wicked way with me, haven't you? Am I right?'

He whispered. 'I haven't... I wouldn't...'

Evelyn, releasing her grip, captured him with a coquettish smile. 'Oh, you wouldn't, would you? We'll see about that. Just you lay back, close your eyes, and relax.'

Her searching fingers twisted the button at his waist and dragged down hard on the zip. As his manhood sprang out, she captured it in her hand. He yelped with pain and pleasure. Releasing the tension in her fingers a little, she maintained a firm grip and swept her hand up and down. Colm moaned. 'My, my, aren't you the biggest of boys!'

The cranking slowed, tightened, quickened and paused. She removed her hand. Dragged away his shorts, underpants, trainers and socks. Cast them into the tall grass at the edge of the clearing. Took him in her hand.

Colm – fit to burst – made to rise. Evelyn pushed him down, held him on the ground.

'Not so quick, Big Boy. Settle down. Relax. We've all the time in the world,' she instructed, 'for foreplay...'

When he could stand it no more, he pushed her off and rolled between her legs. Ravished her with his mouth and tongue, he reached down, dragged her skirt up and peeled off her knickers. Probing her with his fingers, he found her hot and wet.

She felt him poised on the cusp.

'Be gentle. It's my first time.'

Colm smiled, stroked a freckle-dappled cheek, drew a long breath.

'I will. I promise.'

Afterwards, breathless and lathered in sweat, they lay together, her head against his naked chest, his arms enveloping her.

Gazing towards the heavens, he said, 'I'm going home for the summer. Won't be back until the end of September. Did you know?'

'Of course, I know,' she whispered. 'You're all leaving. It's the way of things. Every year the same.'

'And you're not upset?'

'I'll be fine. We'll be fine. Everything will work out for the best.'

He lifted her face to him by the chin and gazed deep into her eyes. Evelyn recognised the sadness in him.

'How can we ever be together?' he said, 'Christ's sake, you're training to be a nun!'

She removed his hand, straddled him with long legs. He felt her moist crotch against his chest. Pinning him down by the shoulders with her knees, she slapped his cheeks playfully. 'Stop it! We can be together. We need to think of your going away as a good thing. *It'll give us both time to think. Time to plan. Time, God willing, for me to leave the order.'*

'You'd do that for me?'

She bent to him, kissed him, pulled away and cupped his face. *'I will. I knew when I first clapped eyes on you, Colm Walsh, things had changed. You're mine. And you always will be.'*

She sank into his embrace. He stroked her hair.

'Come back in September,' she whispered. *'Come back to me. Don't worry, I'll be waiting. Trust me. Do you trust me?'*

He grinned, bit his lip and looked away.

'Well, do you?'

He nibbled her ear. Kissed her freckled cheek.

'Of course, I trust you. I trust every fibre of your being, every bone of your body. I love you, Evelyn. I can't wait for September.'

6

FRIDAY 2ND JANUARY 2015, MIDDAY

The heat-charged air in the interview room hung heavy with sweat, patchouli oil and stale tobacco. Jimmy slouched in a lounge chair and played a mobile between his hands. He wore faded jeans, rubber-capped sneakers, and a washed-to-grey Guns N' Roses t-shirt. A faded Levi jacket hung on the chair behind him. An empty mug and a tatty-edged blue cardboard folder sat within touching distance on the coffee table.

As the door swung open, Jimmy dragged up, sat back, returned his mobile into a hip pocket and turned to DI Alan Wardell and DS David Watts. Stalling, sniffing the air, Wardell studied Jimmy, with circumspection. Dark patches radiating under Jimmy's armpits confirmed Wardell's suspicions.

The three men exchanged polite smiles.

Wardell looked to Watts. 'Open a window, David. It's stifling in here.'

'Yes, boss,' Watts said, rounding the table, cranking a window open, lowering into the chair opposite the aged rocker.

Wardell looked to Jimmy. 'Good afternoon, Mr McNiff. Please, don't get up.'

Wardell and Jimmy shook hands.

'Afternoon,' Jimmy said.

Wardell sat down opposite Jimmy and placed the envelope containing his statement on the table.

'Sorry about the room, it's the only one available, I'm afraid,' Wardell said. 'We've got the decorators in.'

'That's alright, Mr?'

'I'm Detective Inspector Alan Wardell, and this is my colleague, Detective Sergeant David Watts. We're with the Major Crime Unit. You've dropped on, we've a buy one, get one free offer on,' Wardell quipped, smirking.

Jimmy grinned. 'That's a joke, right?'

Not the brightest bulb in the pack, thought Wardell. He nodded, blushed. 'Right. My idea of a joke. My awful sense of humour gets the better of me, sometimes. Take no notice. I'm harmless enough, once the medication kicks in.'

'Not famed for his sense of humour, isn't the Inspector,' Watts said, with a cheesy grin. 'Jimmy Carr needn't worry, eh, boss?'

'I try my best, David,' Wardell replied, pointing at the mug. 'It would be a desperately sad world without humour, wouldn't it? By the way, can I get you another drink, Mr McNiff?'

Jimmy shook his head. 'No, thanks. I'm fine. I had a coffee, not long after I arrived.'

'I'm very glad to hear it.'

Jimmy leaned in, looked to Wardell and Watts. 'I'd prefer it if you called me, Jimmy. Being formal, it's not my thing.'

Wardell nodded. 'OK, Jimmy, shall we make a start on these allegations of yours? It's the reason we're here.'

Jimmy sat back, folded his arms across his chest, drew breath, frowned. 'Yes, let's. It's about time those bastards got their comeuppance. Prison's too good for them.'

Wardell's mouth creased into a conciliatory smile, became serious. 'We'll see... Mr McNiff, sorry, *Jimmy*,' he said. 'I won't lie to you. We're going to have to jump through an awful lot of hoops, before bringing this case to court. Cases of historic child sexual abuse are notoriously difficult to bring to a successful conclusion. That's not to say, we won't give your allegations the attention they deserve. We're going to need to go through your statement in minute detail. It's going to be very painful for you. You're sure you're up to this?'

Jimmy pinched his nostrils, shrugged. 'I've thought long and hard about this, Inspector. It's time to set the record straight. Justice, Inspector, *Sergeant,* that's what I want. Nothing less than justice will do.'

Wardell studied Jimmy. Saw steel in his resolve. Encouraged, he smiled. 'OK. That's excellent,' he said. 'David, take notes, please.'

Nodding, Watts took out a notebook from an inside pocket and turned to a clean page.

Jimmy said, 'Inspector, let's get one thing straight from the off.'

'Alright,' Wardell said.

'These allegations are *real*. They're facts,' exhorted Jimmy, studying and seeking reassurance in the faces of the detectives. 'I'd appreciate it if, from now on, you'd refer to what's written in my statement, as facts. Because, gentlemen, that's precisely what they are. They're facts!'

Wardell studied the wide-eyed Jimmy, looked deep within him. 'Alright, Jimmy, I hear what you say. Your statement, it's factual,' Wardell replied. 'Taking your time, I'd like you to describe the abuse in as much detail as you're able to. I need to know what happened; where it happened; when, and who took part. Take a break whenever you feel the need.'

Jimmy flipped open the blue folder. 'I thought you'd say that,

Inspector. So, I've prepared a schedule of dates, times, names and things.'

'Things?' Wardell asked.

'Things they did, or made me do. My memory isn't what it once was. There's a lot to remember. More even to forget. I kept a diary from the age of fourteen. By then, I knew what they were doing wasn't right. Everything that happened – the abuse – is described on the schedule. Everything that is, that I can remember. The others, Niall and Colm, they might remember more. You'd have to ask them yourself.'

Jimmy lifted stapled sheets from the blue folder and handed a copy each to Wardell and Watts, keeping a copy for himself. Wardell mouthed a 'thank you,' David Watts, a 'cheers.' Jimmy returned the surplus copies to the folder. Wardell counted the sheets. There were four in total.

Jimmy said, 'The dates and times are approximate, except, of course, those when I kept a diary. Before I kept a diary, I can't give exact dates. They're my best guess. I was ten when it started. It's forty years ago. Everything's scheduled out. I think about what they did every waking hour. At night, I have nightmares like you wouldn't believe.'

Jimmy's dark eyes moistened. Sniffling, he wiped the underside of his nose with the back of his hand and gazed towards the floor.

Wardell scan read the list. Noticed particular words repeated innumerable times: masturbate; touched; stroked; oral; cane, and detention. The schedule read as a litany of the worst kind of abuse. The names of the alleged abusers highlighted in bold against each allegation.

Wardell set the papers on the table, looked to Jimmy. 'Thanks, Jimmy. This is very useful. I'm afraid we need to hear you describe in your own words what happened. I appreciate it will be painful. Our role is to build a credible case for the prosecution based on facts that will stand up in a court of law. We need to present the strongest case we can to the Crown Prosecution Service. It's they that we need to convince there's a case to answer to. Only then will they – the CPS – move forward with a prosecution. We'll sit and listen,' Wardell said, pointing to the video camera hung on the wall below the ceiling. 'Just so you're aware. As a matter of course, we record everything. Is that OK?'

Jimmy swallowed hard. 'I suppose so.'

'Good. Over the next month, we'll gather and corroborate as much evidence as possible.'

'And recording everything is absolutely necessary, I take it?'

'Yes, I'm afraid it is. The case will succeed or fail on the strength of the evidence. Shout when you need a break.'

Jimmy slurped on lukewarm coffee, cleared his throat with a cough. 'Right, let's get started.'

7

FRIDAY 2ND JANUARY 2015, 12.15 P.M

'I don't know where to begin,' Jimmy said.

'At the beginning?' Watts suggested.

Wardell glared.

'I'm sorry,' Watts said, 'ignore me.'

'That's alright, Sergeant. I was young and daft once,' Jimmy said, raising a mirthful smile from Wardell. Watts's face flushed pomegranate red.

'The beginning,' Jimmy reaffirmed, 'The abuse started the week after my parents dropped me off at St Aubert's. It was the second week of September 1970. I was fast asleep in the dormitory. Myself, Billy, Niall and Colm shared a four-bed dorm. I'd slept in. I remember being alone. O'Connell appeared at the side of my bed. He must've assumed I was asleep. But I wasn't. I was pretending. My eyes were half closed. He bent down and put his mouth against my ear. Even now, I can still smell his manky breath. It was a mixture of halitosis and cigarettes. It was revolting. I almost vomited. I got the same feeling you get when a dog breathes on your face. Felt like I wanted to chuck. Somehow, I controlled the urge. He must've known I was awake. I held it down. Without warning, he screamed into my ear, "Wake up, lazy gobshite! Or you'll be late for prayers". I almost jumped out of my skin. I fell out and rolled under the bed. Remember, I was only ten. O'Connell reached under the bed and dragged me out by the hair. He lifted me up by the scruff, threw me against the wall and kicked my legs out from under me. I landed on the floor so hard, I almost lost consciousness. I curled up. He went berserk and laced into me. As luck would have it, he was wearing pumps. He wore pumps a lot – those rubber-soled black ones the teachers used to make us wear for PE. He kicked the shit out of me. Eventually, he got tired and stopped. When he'd got his breath back, he screamed at me like a maniac, "Get dressed! I want you downstairs in one minute, or you're going to feel the back of my hand!" He was drooling like a man possessed. His eyes were literally popping out of his head. Suddenly, he fell silent. After about a minute, he said, "Blab to the others, and you'll feel my belt across your backside. I'll hit you so hard, you'll not be able to sit down for a week". Not long after he'd attacked me, Colm confided in me how O'Connell had attacked him, too. Told me how he'd knocked him out cold for ripping his shirt in the playground playing football one dinner time. For years after O'Connell's attack, Colm suffered memory loss and panic attacks. Niall and Billy said O'Connell would beat them whenever he got the opportunity. We all had bruises to prove it. The sadistic bastard loved inflicting pain. I remember Billy showing me his backside. It was black and blue all over. In hindsight, the abuse was about control. About power. I suppose it must've given him some kind of perverted gratification. The Church empowered his sadistic streak. Sad fuck. Scrub that. Sad *fucks*. We lived in a perpetual state of fear, wondering when he, or Murphy, would come calling? What mood they'd be in? What they'd do; want? How bad it would be?'

Jimmy fell silent, tears welled in his eyes. He stared at the table top.

'Are you alright?' Wardell asked. 'We'll take a break if you like?'

Jimmy looked up, shook his head. 'No, I'm OK. I need this story told. Get it off my chest.'

'So long as you're sure?'

'Yeah, I'm sure. So... Just when I thought it couldn't get any worse, that's when the sexual abuse started. It started with a quick grope in a corridor. I'd turn around and he'd be standing there – O'Connell – with a sick, fucked-up grin on his face. He'd raise a finger across his mouth and whisper, *"Jimmy, think on... What happens between you and me is our little secret. You must never tell another living soul about it. You know that, don't you?"* The abuse stepped up a gear. He'd touch me up in the showers. Lather me with soap, paying particular attention to my genitals. It was only possible because he made us shower alone. He'd abuse us whenever he got the chance. It was my first, I hesitate to say it, sexual experience. They're sick fuckers: O'Connell, Murphy, and the nuns. The nuns, they turned a blind eye.'

'One time – O'Connell and Murphy – attacked me together. One night, they came into the dorm in the early hours. In full view of the others, they dragged me out of bed and frogmarched me to O'Connell's study. I tried to resist, but I was a skinny twelve-year-old against two grown men. What chance did I have? I'll tell you what chance I had... I had no chance. They reeked of spirits – whisky and brandy. Pissed, but compos mentis. There's no doubt in my mind that they'd planned it together. They had me sit down between them on the sofa and put a porn video on. They made me play with them. Murphy came first. I threw up. They laughed their heads off. It was revolting. The abuse spiralled out of control. It got much worse. Dirty bastards.'

'Then, when I was thirteen, they moved me into a single

room. It gave them the privacy they craved. The privacy to abuse me whenever they got the urge. They'd bring alcohol: whisky; spirits; cans of lager. Sometimes, strong cider and ply me with drink, either together or alone. I tried to resist. I spat it out. I took a beating for doing that. The punishment was the cane or a slipper across my backside. Pissed out of my brain, they'd take it in turns to sodomise me. It happened three, maybe four, times a month for two years. I got used to it. I grew accustomed to their visits. Hated them. But there was nothing I could do.'

'They shared me. I was their plaything. Everyone knew what was going on. We were too scared to tell our parents. The threats they made were real, not idle. After a while, I, *we*, blocked it out. We couldn't even bring ourselves to talk about it with one another. We'd nowhere to go. Physically... Psychologically... We were imprisoned inside our heads by fear. The nuns knew what was going on. They slapped us down if we said anything. Vicious cows. They were as bad as the priests.'

'I felt hollowed out. It was a hopeless situation. I contemplated suicide: thought about it all the time. Most nights, I'd lay in a comatose state. I had this reoccurring dream. In it, I imagined stealing a rowing boat from the bay and rowing far out to sea and throwing myself overboard. I'd see myself sinking deeper and deeper into the sea, arms and legs outstretched. A human starfish made of lead. My mouth would be wide open and I'd be swallowing gallons of seawater. I savoured it. Drank it in. The deeper I sank, the more I swallowed, I became calmer and calmer. When I reached the bottom, I'd see myself laid in a coffin surrounded by crucifixes scattered across the sand – hundreds of them. My face as white as milk, eyelids closed. O'Connell would swim down, tread water over me, cross my arms over my chest and make the sign of the cross. There would be an explosion and he'd disappear in a cloud of sand. I had this overwhelming feeling of joy. Of release. Of joy at being dead. But it was only a dream.'

'Then, just when I thought things couldn't get any worse, they did. O'Connell showed me something in his study. Something I'll never forget. It was a boiling hot summer day in August 1976, not long after my sixteenth birthday.'

'What did he show you?' Wardell asked, perched on the edge of the seat.

'I helped him remove floorboards in his study. He reached into the floor void, took out a dusty Quality Street tin, placed it on the desk and told me to sit next to him. He prised the lid off. It opened with a pop. There was a foul smell. Best I can liken it to, is musty football boots after you've stepped in dog shit. Inside...' McNiff caught his breath. His doleful eyes connected with Wardell's and told of his pain. 'Inside were the remains of a baby – a male foetus. It was tiny. About the size of a starling. I couldn't stop staring at it, I'd never seen anything like it.'

'You're sure it was a boy?'

'Yeah, you could make out the genitals under the umbilical cord.'

'And the mother and father? Who were they?' Wardell asked.

Uncertainty flitted across Jimmy's face. He shrugged. 'O'Connell told me the mother was a nun. A novice nun called Evelyn. He said that the baby was the bastard product of a liaison between Evelyn and the gardener's son. Told me Murphy had aborted the baby because it was God's will. That God worked in mysterious ways. That I should take heed. He warned me I'd suffer the same fate if ever I told anyone about our special relationship. Bastard held a blade against my Adam's apple. It drew blood. He said he'd warned the others. Warned us all to keep our mouths shut, forever. Added, he'd come looking for us, if we ever said anything to anyone.'

'You must've been petrified?'

'I was. I can still feel the knife against my throat all these years later.' Jimmy's right hand rose to his windpipe. 'It's taken me till now, till I'm 54 years of age, to tell another living soul about any of this. Billy's alleged suicide being the catalyst. It's the reason I've plucked up the courage to come forward. Poor Billy. No way did he commit suicide.'

'Billy?' Wardell queried.

'Billy Searle. He's an old school friend. He was abused, too. Someone murdered Billy last week. You lot reckon it was suicide, but it wasn't. Billy would never take his life.'

Wardell's eyebrows raised. 'OK, Jimmy, we'll look into that.'

'Make sure you do.'

'This baby – the foetus in the tin – do you have any idea how they got rid of it?' Watts asked.

'I know exactly where he put it.'

'You do?' Wardell said.

'Yes, I do. I helped him put it there.'

'Where?'

'Under the floorboards within the floor void.'

'You did?'

'Yes, I did. He made me. That's another reason he asked me to his study that day. Not just to threaten me, but to help him. He needed someone to help him lift and replace the floorboards. The whole of the right alcove next to the chimney breast. It's probably still there. Christ knows?'

'Oh my God!' Watts exclaimed

'If only there was a God, Sergeant, then none of this would ever have happened.'

Jimmy looked to the floor, shook, blubbered. His cries increased to deep belly sobs.

Wardell settled a hand on Jimmy's shoulder and offered what little solace he could.

8

SATURDAY 3RD JANUARY 2015, 10.00 A.M

The tanned, bald man sat in the rental van's sultry interior watching a wall of dispiriting grey fog roll in off the sea. Studying his reflection mirrored on the inside of the windscreen, he sighed, reached forward and turned off the heater. As the motor fell silent, he reached up and twisted the two top buttons of his overalls, open.

It was a wet and dismal winter morning. He loathed such mornings. Despised how the weather sucked the life out of people. He remembered his life before. How he'd hankered to live anywhere but England in winter. Home was the Costa Del Sol. He made that commitment. Would see out his days under the scorching Mediterranean sun. England, and grim English winters, could go hang.

But work was work, a necessary evil, whatever the country, whatever the season. "Son, you've got to follow the work", his father had told him. "Do that, and you'll never starve". And so he had. He also understood his father would never regard what he did as *work*.

His mind wandered to the lucrative business at hand. To the

brief telephone conversation with Salvatore – the Bishop's right-hand man. Salvatore paid well, and on the nail. Would sometimes, as now, demand his pound of flesh. The deal simple: no flesh, no payment. Salvatore's valued custom would often require trips to the UK in winter. Annoying though it was, pissing Salvatore off wasn't a viable option – not if seeing another day dawn was high on a person's list of priorities.

Plan. Focus. Deliver. His personal mantra rallied through his head.

This time, Salvatore demanded photographic and physical evidence. The photographic evidence already secured. The tongues were a work-in-progress. He supposed the tongues were symbolic. But of what? He saw little point dwelling on such matters.

Time dragging, he glanced at his wristwatch. Ahead, a dirt-brown seagull soared across his line of sight, swooped down, landed on the pavement opposite and collected a meaty chip, half covered in blood-red ketchup. With the chip lodged between its beak, it took to the air, chased into the murk by an angry crow. The deep bass burp of a distant foghorn echoed along the shore. A car raced past, sending a sheen of muddy rainwater lashing against the car window.

England in winter: Godforsaken.

He drew a long breath, exhaled through his nose and wiped the underside of his nose with a handkerchief. So far, he had waited four long hours with nothing to show for his patience. Four hours, staring at the same door on the flats ten metres away. He closed his eyes and saw the image of the blue, sun-bleached door imprinted on his retinas.

He checked his phone. Nothing: no missed calls, texts, or emails. Nobody, it seemed, loved him today. Nobody would, were they to know the reason for his visit.

His mind wandered to Spain. There, it had just gone eleven,

the burning sun climbing inexorably into a perfect cerulean sky, over the shimmering azure Med. He imagined Jessica, settling on a sunbed by the pool, expensive tits straining against the nylon chrome-look, bikini, golden skin glistening with oil, manicured nails collecting the first pink gin of the day. How he craved to be there: not in England under leaden skies in a claustrophobic metal box, labelled with a blue oval.

Come on! Come on! he ranted.

Shuffling onto the edge of the seat squab, he settled atop the steering wheel and gazed at the block of flats. He closed his eyes, opened them in time to see a curtain twitch in an upstairs window. A man – naked from the waist up – dragged the curtains open, revealed his shoulder length grey-licked hair, pastel white skin and emaciated build.

An audible sigh of relief escaped the tanned man's lips, and he smiled a thin smile.

After five minutes, stirring, he looked in the passenger door mirror and saw parked cars, an elderly woman in a long purple coat dragging a shopping trolley, a street sweeper in orange oilskins, and a mangy tabby cat sat on a car bonnet looking out to sea. He collected a photograph of James 'Jimmy' McNiff from the centre console and lay it across the steering wheel. Smoothing the edges, he studied Jimmy's craggy face and decided it was the same man who had opened the curtains moments earlier.

Returning the photograph to a breast pocket, he dragged on the door handle, rolled out onto the pavement and meandered to the rear. There, he swung open the back doors. Straightening, yawning, he spun his gaze around. Satisfied his arrival had gone unnoticed, he set off towards the blue door.

At the gate to the block of flats, he sat down on a low brick wall enclosing a paved area. Balanced on the concrete coping, he felt the silenced Beretta under his palm. He looked out to sea, biding his time.

Two minutes later, sensing movement in the corner of his left eye, he nudged the Beretta's safety catch off. Behind him, he heard hinges creak, a Yale lock click, footsteps and the garden gate opening. Beside him, the low timber gate sprung open, then clattered closed and a slim, long-haired man in jeans, tatty denim jacket and dirty sneakers appeared. Their eyes met. A nod passed between them. A polite half-smile exchanged. An identification made.

Jimmy uncoupled his eyes from the stranger and swung left towards Whitby, and the rental van parked with the rear doors open at the side of the road.

The tanned, bald man fell in step behind him, shoulders stooped against the mizzle.

Closing.

Gaining.

Timing and quickening his step.

Parallel with the back of the van – the open doors – he barged past Jimmy and spun around, blocking the pavement.

'Excuse me, mate,' said the bald man in broad Cockney.

Jimmy slid to a halt. 'Can I help you?'

Two feet lay between them.

'Don't I know you?'

'I don't think so,' Jimmy replied, shaking his head. 'You're confusing me with someone else. Sorry, I'd love to stop and chat, only I've got to run.'

The bald man glared, fell silent. Jimmy, sensing something amiss, studied him through narrowed eyes. Confused, a sense of uncertainty – of fear – roiled through him.

'That's it, you're James McNiff. I recognise you.'

'Who wants to know?'

'Me. You're coming with me, my old mush.'

Jimmy, sniggering, stepped right. 'I don't think so.'

The bald man moved forward. So close that Jimmy could feel

his breath warm against his face. The glare morphed to a devilish glower.

'Don't fuck with me.'

Something tubular settled into Jimmy's gut and firm palm at the bottom of his spine. 'Ouch! What the fuck's got into you, mate? You on something, or what? What do you want? What's this about?'

'Shut it. Get in the van.' The bald man nodded at the open doors. 'And no, I'm not on something. Bloody Yorkshire pudding. Drugs are for losers. Losers like you. So why don't you be a good lad and do as you're told. Get in.'

Jimmy plunged his hands deep into jacket pockets. 'Whatever... I haven't got time for this bullshit. Excuse me,' Jimmy said, stepping right.

A stab in the kidneys.

'Ouch! That hurt!' Jimmy yelped. 'You bastard! C'mon let's have it.'

The man snarled. 'Easy tiger. If I were you, I'd reconsider your last statement.' Jimmy, feeling the pressure in his guts release, looked down and saw the gun. 'That, my friend, is precision Italian engineering. It's a silenced Beretta. One shot will turn your guts into spaghetti. It's a beautiful thing. You're trying my patience. I'm going to ask you one last time... Get. Into. The. Back. Of. The. Fucking! Van! Either do as I say, or take your last breath. It's your call.' He glowered, shrugged. 'Either way, I ain't fussed.'

Jimmy raised his hands. 'OK... OK,' he said, stepping left. 'Relax,' he said, clambering into the van.

9

MONDAY 1ST SEPTEMBER 1975

Summer drew its last breath and became autumn. And with autumn came the start of a new academic year at St Aubert's Boarding School for Boys. The woods surrounding the school burned fiery reds, rampant oranges and incandescent yellows under slate grey and occasional blue skies. A cacophony of noise and young life returned to the school.

Evelyn had yearned for Colm's return. Longed to hold him again. To hold him close. Confide in him. Share her secret. Love him. And together, God willing, plan their escape.

10

MONDAY 8TH SEPTEMBER 1975, 10.00 A.M

Sister Mary O'Toole's scowling, time-weathered face appeared in the door opening. Two bulging hessian sacks sat on the floor at her feet. 'Sister Evelyn, shake a leg. It's time you were out of that pit of yours,' she barked. 'I need a hand with these tatties.'

Evelyn placed the leather-bound copy of the Holy Bible on the bedside table and eased out of bed.

'There's no time to dawdle. Shake a leg.'

'I'm sorry, Sister,' Evelyn said, slipping on a veil, tucking auburn hair in under the white material.

Colm Walsh stood against the corridor wall, his leg bent at the knee, foot balanced on the smooth stone. Hearing the rattle of footsteps across parquet, he looked left along the corridor and saw two nuns carrying sacks. As the nuns approached, Colm launched from the wall and the nuns halted. A smiling Colm stole a glance at Evelyn. Their eyes connected. Evelyn, eyelids batting, looked away.

'Morning Sister O'Toole. Evelyn. Beautiful day don't you think?'

A frowning O'Toole lowered the sack to the floor and folded her arms under her bosom. 'Shouldn't you be in a lesson?'

'First lesson is after lunch. Latin, followed by English.'

O'Toole tutted. 'Do something productive, why don't you? Hanging around in corridors will get you nowhere, Colm Walsh. You realise that, don't you?'

Colm gave a blank look and stood aside. O'Toole gave Colm the evil eye, collected the sack and set off at a march. As Evelyn approached, Colm tripped and fell forward. A surprised Evelyn cast out a steadying hand, broke Colm's fall.

'Here, let me help you,' Evelyn said, raising Colm by the elbow.

'Thank you, Sister. What a clumsy oaf I am. I tripped over my own feet...'

Evelyn's flaring eyes settled on Colm's left breast pocket.

'Yes... Well... What can I say? So long as you're alright,' Evelyn said. 'There's no harm done.'

A scowling O'Toole beckoned Evelyn. 'Keep up, Evelyn. I'm sure the clumsy eejit can look after himself.'

At the end of the corridor, O'Toole halted and spun around to Evelyn, eyes ablaze with anger. 'Is he the one?' she barked. 'Don't you dare lie. Lying will do you no good. Well? Is he?'

Evelyn feigned indignation. 'No, Sister, he is not. Whatever gave you that idea?'

'Are you sure about that? You're certain he's not the miscreant?'

'Yes.'

O'Toole's thin lips puckered into a sour pout. 'You're aware telling lies is a mortal sin in the eyes of the Lord? That it is an abomination of the very worst kind.'

'I'm aware of that, yes, Sister.'

'And keeping the father's name secret is such an abomination?'

Evelyn's eyes rolled to the ceiling. O'Toole slapped Evelyn's face. 'Don't you dare look away when I'm talking to you. Look at me, girl!'

Evelyn faced O'Toole with wild eyes, lips quivering, jaw set firm.

O'Toole exhaled an exaggerated sigh. 'Evelyn, I don't understand you. This continuing silence, this lie of yours, is despicable. You're an absolute disgrace. May the one true Almighty Lord have mercy on your soul come Judgement Day. C'mon. These tatties will be rotten by the time they're delivered.'

Colm recovered the slip of paper from a breast pocket. Evelyn's handwritten message was brief.

meet me at the bridge at five tonight. Don't you dare be late... x

* * *

Evelyn arrived at the beck ten minutes past the hour. Colm stood on the bridge lobbing sticks into the water. Sensing movement, hearing the rustle of undergrowth, he turned to Evelyn with open arms.

Evelyn fell into his arms. 'Sorry, I'm late. O'Toole's been watching me like a hawk all day. Rotten bloody cow, she is.'

Colm pulled Evelyn to him. Embraced her. They kissed. Evelyn pushed from him, spun, leaned on the parapet and cried. Her tears splashed into the bubbling beck and ran off with the current.

Colm lifted her chin. 'Eh, stop that. Please, don't cry. I don't *like to see you upset,' he cooed. 'We're together now. I've missed you so much, Evelyn. You're all I've thought about all summer.'*

Evelyn faced him, lips trembling into a weak smile. She blew her nose on a handkerchief, wiped tears off of her cheeks and from the corners of her eyes. She swallowed hard. 'There's something important I need to tell you. It can't wait any longer. C'mon. Let's sit on the log.'

Her voice sounded hollow, broken. Something in it filled him with dread. Something he had never heard before.

Colm collected Evelyn's hand.

'Before you say anything... There's something I need to know...' Colm's glare bore into her.

'What?' Evelyn said.

'Have they interfered with you? Because if they have, as God is my judge, I'll kill them with my bare hands.'

He saw relief behind her eyes, in the set of her face. 'Shh,' she said, placing a finger across his lips. 'No, it's nothing like that. They wouldn't dare. Not with me, they wouldn't. Please, Colm, let's go sit on the log.'

She led him from the bridge onto the gravel bank. Ten yards upstream they came to their special place – a moss-covered tree trunk laid on its side, fanned by ferns. They sat within touching distance. Colm kissed Evelyn's forehead. She inhaled a long breath. A glazed look foretold anguish.

Two minutes passed.

'What's a matter? You're worrying me. You seem so sad?'

She turned to him, looked deep into his eyes. 'Colm, promise not hate me...'

'Ugh? Hate you? How could I ever hate you? What's this all about, Evelyn? What's so important that you think I'll hate you?' he said. 'You're out of your gorgeous Irish mind if you think I'll ever be able to hate you, to be sure you are,' he said in a faux Irish lilt, grinning.

She held his hand. 'While you were away, I was sick every morning.'

'Alright? And?'

'And, it got so bad, I had to tell them. I was showing, anyway. They took me to the doctor in Whitby. It was the first week of August. The doctor – Doctor Bryan – he did some tests.'

'Evelyn, I'm not being funny... Only... Where are you going with this? I'm confused.'

'The tests, Colm, they came back positive.'

'Tests? What tests? I don't understand.'

'Colm! Stop it! Stop being thick! The tests, the ones Doctor Bryan did, they were pregnancy tests.'

Colm's mouth fell agog. 'Oh...'

'The tests confirmed I was three months gone.'

Colour draining from his face, he bolted up and stepped over to the beck. After a silent minute, he turned to Evelyn, expression twisted with shock and confusion.

'Am I going to be a father?'

She looked at him with sad eyes. 'No, Colm,' she paused, 'you're not.'

He moved towards her. 'I'm confused. One minute you're pregnant, then you're not. What's going on? Is this a joke? If it is, it's a sick one.'

'It's no joke. I'd never joke about something of such impor-tance. What do you take me for?'

Colm swallowed hard. 'I know... I know... I'm sorry... I shouldn't have said that. Only...'

Staring at the gravel, she launched a stick into the beck with her right boot. Hollered. Sobbed.

'What's going on? I need to know. I've every right to know.'

Her doleful eyes met his. 'Please don't make this any harder than it already is. Don't make a scene. Please sit down.'

He lowered himself onto the trunk.

'I'm sorry, I shouldn't have raised my voice. You're hurting. Tell me everything, Evelyn. Every damn thing.'

She reached out, took his hand.

'He was a perfect baby boy, so tiny, but I swear I could see you in him. He had the most gorgeous wee face. I named him Thomas. He was perfect.' Evelyn stalled, tears welling in her eyes. 'Colm, I'm so very sorry...'

He put his arm around her shoulders, pulled him to her. 'C'mon, stop that. I'm here now.'

She pushed him away, looked to him with tears in her eyes.

'They drugged me and aborted our baby without my consent. I was powerless. Whatever drug they made me take, I couldn't move. All I could do was lay there and watch them kill our son. Colm, listen to what I'm saying. I watched them take our son away. I watched him die. He was too young to live. I'm sorry, Colm. Your son, he's gone. They snuffed his life out. If only they'd taken me instead...'

11

SUNDAY 4TH JANUARY 2015, 6.30 P.M.

After a fairly uneventful day, DI Alan Wardell decided to call it a day. With a fair wind, he would arrive home for the start of the news. Checking the time, he yawned and stretched. Shuffling into a Crombie, he set off for the stairwell. Passing through the office, Wardell said breezy goodbyes to the few remaining detectives, hunched over their desks.

Entering reception, Wardell's gaze tracked left toward Desk Sergeant Willie Dale. Dale's hangdog expression never seemed to change or betray his mood.

'Night, Willie. Have a quiet one,' Wardell said with a smile.

Dale, recognising Wardell, sat back, scanned the line of post-it notes stuck to the desk. 'Before you go,' he said, collecting a note. 'Can I have a word, Alan?'

Inside, Wardell died a little more. Removing his hand from the door handle, he spun on his heels and stepped over to the reception desk. 'What's up, Willie? You look a bit miffed.'

'I'm a tad annoyed.'

'Why? Nothing I've done, hopefully.'

'This last half hour, I've been trying to contact someone in Major Crimes Unit, but nobody picked up. Phones kept ringing out. I tried anyone and everyone.'

Wardell shrugged, gave Dale a blank look. 'Sorry, Willie, I expect the phones are playing up again. Would explain why it's been so quiet, today. Bloody useless they are. I'll arrange for an engineer to give them the once over first thing tomorrow morning. Why did you want to speak to someone in MCU?'

Dale lifted the post-it. 'Half an hour ago, I fielded a call from Whitby. They wanted to speak to one of your lot. They reckon they've got a murder on their patch out Sandsend way. Do you know it? Sandsend?'

'I can't say that I do.'

'It's a hamlet two miles north of Whitby, out on the coast road. I holidayed there as a kid. Stayed in a static on the clifftop overlooking the beach. We...'

Wardell wondered where Dale was going with his reminiscences, interjected, 'Sorry to interrupt, Willie. Did Whitby give any details?'

Willie nodded. 'Some, yes.'

'And?'

'Uniform attended a flat in Sandsend late on this afternoon. They found a body. A Caucasian male in his fifties. Poor sod received two gunshot wounds to the head. No weapon found at the scene. No evidence of a disturbance. And, Alan, there's something else.'

'Go on.'

'The victim's tongue...'

'What about it?'

'Cut out.'

'Christ. No?'

'I'm afraid so. The DC that called – a DC Yvonne Millen –

she called direct from the locus. She sounded shook up. Uniform visited the address after a friend popped in and found the deceased tied to a chair with his tongue removed, seemingly post mortem. SOCO, the Crime Scene Photographer and the Doctor are already on site. Miss Phelan is en route as we speak. The locus is secure. SOCOs seem happy enough.'

Sandsend pondered Wardell. It seemed familiar, but why? It came to him in a blinding flash. James McNiff lived in Sandsend.

'Do we have the identities of the persons registered to the address?' Wardell asked.

'Just one person. One James McNiff. He's a bingo caller in Whitby.'

'He lived alone?'

'According to the electoral register, yes.'

Dale handed Wardell the post-it with DC Millen's mobile number and McNiff's address scribbled on it.

'DC Millen is expecting someone to return her call. You'll need the address.'

Wardell released an involuntary sigh, ground his teeth. His evening by the TV, feet up, frustrated.

Wardell accepted the note, nodded. 'Thanks, Willie. Did you see DS Watts step out of the door? He left about ten minutes ago?'

'No, sir. He mentioned in passing, he was nipping down to the canteen for a coffee. Mumbled something about a nice young lady. He was grinning like the Cheshire Cat.'

Wardell rolled his eyes. 'Dirty young pup. I'd better find him. Seems, me and the lothario Watts, are going to the seaside,' Wardell said, heading off toward the stairs to the basement canteen. 'There'd better be a chip shop open, when we get there.'

* * *

Wardell and Watts arrived in Whitby as the winter day-trippers were leaving town. A long line of traffic crawled up the steep hill heading south. Far below, in the valley bottom, the River Esk divided the town into two unequal parts. On the north bank sat the bulk of the built-up area. Opposite, and across the river, high on the headland, stood the impressive floodlit gothic abbey. The ink-black river dividing the town shimmered with a million reflections. Flashing green and red lights marked the entrance to the harbour.

Wardell had slept for the entire journey.

'Boss!' Watts barked, leaning left, nudging Wardell in the ribs.

Wardell stirred, grunted and dragged upright. Rubbing his eyes, adjusting his clothing, he yawned.

'Boss, Whitby,' Watts said, nodding in the direction of the town. 'On the right in the valley bottom. Three miles, and we'll be there.'

'Good,' Wardell said, flattening his hair.

'Stunning at night don't you think?' Watts said.

Wardell suppressed another yawn under a fist, glanced past Watts. 'Oh yeah... Whitby... At night... Amazing...'

Passing into open country, distant strobes of electric blue, neon red and orange light divided the dark night sky ahead.

'Reckon those lights are Sandsend, David?'

'Must be.'

Three miles and five minutes later, the Mondeo rounded a bend and the view ahead opened out. The road meandered down a hillside towards a melee of vehicles parked inside a cordon bounded by blue and white 'POLICE DO NOT CROSS' tape. Two uniformed PCs ordered traffic to complete U-turns at either end of the cordon.

Watts brought the Mondeo to a halt alongside the PC guarding the northern end of the cordon. A hooded face, streaked with rain, appeared at the passenger door glass. Wardell lowered the glass and flipped open his warrant card.

'DI Wardell and DS Watts from the Major Crime Unit based out of Harrogate. We're here for the evening performance. Has the curtain gone up, yet?'

The PC smirked, sniffled. 'I'm afraid so, sir. SOCO were keen to make a start.' The PC stole a glance at his wristwatch. 'There's an intermission in an hour,' replied the young PC, enjoying the banter, lifting the tape. 'Park close to the vans, gentlemen. Enjoy the show, but please, no flash photography, or mobile telephones.'

A smirking Wardell gave the PC the thumbs up and raised the glass.

Watts drifted the Mondeo forward and parked as instructed. They stepped out of the car. Watts collected a plastic box from the boot, closed the boot lid and strode over to the entrance to the flats. A young woman in a dark trouser suit and high heels sat on a low wall with a grey blanket draped around her shoulders. In her right hand, she clutched a takeaway coffee in a paper cup. Even under the sodium wash of street lamps, Wardell noticed her face was bereft of colour.

'DC Millen?'

'That's right.'

'DI Wardell, DC Watts, from MCU, Harrogate. You happy if we take over?'

'Try delighted.'

'It's that bad?'

'The worst I've seen by a considerable margin.'

'I see. Has the doctor been yet?'

'Yes. Been and gone. Certified the victim dead an hour back. He's estimated time of death as between ten to twelve hours ago. Which suggests he was murdered sometime between ten a.m. and midday, today.'

'I see,' Wardell nodded. 'Need I ask, likely cause?'

Millen smirked. Mumbled something indecipherable under her breath. Shook her head and looked away. Looked back. Re-engaged with Wardell. 'Gunshot. Sorry, *gunshots*. Poor bastard was shot twice in the head from close range. The killer tied him to a chair and despatched him. Professional job, I reckon. All the hallmarks are present. There's two neat gunshot wounds on the left temple, an inch apart.' Millen mimicked a handgun with her right hand. 'Pow! Pow! The presence of soot blackening around the entrance wounds, indicates the barrel was in contact with his skin. Neighbours never heard a thing. It suggests the gun was equipped with a silencer. It indicates a level of professionalism, and premeditation.'

'Let's not get ahead of ourselves, Detective,' Wardell said, adding. 'Something about a tongue?'

'Excised. Removed. Cut out. No sign of it anywhere. Also, it wasn't the neatest of jobs. The kitchen floor looks like a scene from The Texas Chainsaw Massacre. It's horrible. You'll see.'

Wardell glanced at Watts, eyebrows raised. 'Thank you, DC Millen, an excellent synopsis. You've done more than enough. Finish your drink, then get off home.'

Millen nodded, sipped coffee. 'I will. And thanks. The paperwork will be on your desk first thing tomorrow morning.'

'Don't worry about it. There's no rush. Get it done when you're feeling up to it. Midday will suffice.'

'Thanks, sir.'

Wardell and Watts stepped away. Watts set the plastic box down on the concrete slabs, sank onto his haunches and clicked the lid open.

'I thought on, boss,' Watts said.

'Good man.'

They put on disposable overalls, overshoes, face masks and

pulled on hair nets and latex gloves. As they dressed, spasmodic camera flashes illuminated the block of flats.

'Ready?' Wardell said, voice muffled by the mask.

Watts dipped his head. 'As I'll ever be.'

SOCOs had marked a safe route into the flat with tape. The two detectives climbed the staircase, taking care not to touch the handrail. McNiff lived in a first-floor flat, one of six converted from a fisherman's cottage.

Arriving on the first floor landing, a burly SOC officer leant against the door jamb, studying his phone. Wardell recognised him. 'Well, well, well, if it isn't Kenny Goddard. Fancy seeing you here,' Wardell said.

'Well, hello, Alan Wardell,' Goddard said, lowering the phone, looking over Wardell's left shoulder, nodding, 'and David Watts. Aren't we the privileged ones? We get to enjoy an all-expenses paid trip to the seaside, on a freezing cold winter night?'

The three men shook rubber-gloved hands.

'Quite,' Wardell said, stepping back. 'Making progress, Kenny?'

Kenny nodded. 'Fair to say we are, yes. When you get the chance, give my compliments to uniform and that lovely young DC who secured the scene. Between them, they've done a sterling job. So far, I haven't noticed any contamination.'

'I will. The victim is still in situ then, Kenny?' Wardell asked, nodding past Goddard.

'That's right, Alan. Would you gents like the guided tour now? The photographer's finishing up. That's the reason I'm taking a break. I don't want to get immortalised in pixels.'

'If it's no trouble?'

'No trouble at all. It will be my pleasure,' Goddard said, with a trace of hesitation. 'One thing, before we go in.'

'What?'

'Did anyone say anything about the poor man's tongue?'

'DC Millen mentioned it, yes.'

Goddard's expression morphed from concern to relief. 'Good. Good. Sadly, it's gone AWOL. The tongue, I mean. Not a trace of it anywhere. It's a tad annoying. It might have told us something,' Goddard said, lips upturned into a sickly grin, a sparkle in his eye.

Wardell grimaced. Watts looked away, bit his lip.

'I'm sorry, Alan. David. Gallows humour. I'm afraid it's an occupational hazard. Too often it gets the better of me. That was very insensitive of me. Scrub that. Actually, it was rather sick. Ah well, mustn't grumble. Tongue, or no tongue, we'll make do with what we've got.'

Wardell nodded. 'You do that, Kenny. I'm told Miss Phelan is on her way?'

'Yes, Alan. Truth is, she took a wee while to answer my call. Seems she was dining out with a friend. She's hoping to arrive around midnight.'

Wardell nodded. 'Let's get this over with, time and tide and all that. I'll catch up with her at the post mortem.'

The three men stepped into a simple lounge-cum-dining room. From the lounge, two doors led off to the bedroom and kitchen. AC/DC, Status Quo and Black Sabbath tour posters adorned the walls. A 3D pop-art oil painting of Lemmy from Motorhead hung on the wall above an ancient electric bar fire. Tatty-edged copies of Kerrang lay scattered across the floor. A threadbare floral print, mahogany-spindled sofa sat central in the room. The sofa faced a super-sized TV. A pine table sat against the back wall. The none too subtle pungent aroma of marijuana seemed to seep from the floor, walls and ceiling. A bingo caller's wage didn't appear to stretch very far in the charity shops of a North Yorkshire seaside town, thought Wardell.

A hubbub of SOCOs milled around the kitchen. Two uniformed officers sat at a table drinking tea and munching on

Rich Tea biscuits. The police photographer shouldered his way through the SOCOs and said his goodbyes.

Kenny Goddard stood in the kitchen door opening, cleared his throat.

Everyone turned.

'Stand aside, everyone. The cavalry has arrived.'

12

MONDAY 5TH JANUARY 2015, 8.10 A.M

Wardell entered the investigation room, halted by the table, and confirmed everyone who needed to be present was, in fact, present. Steering his gaze to each person, everyone returned a gesture of acknowledgement. Satisfied, he ambled over to the head of the table and set down an inch-thick blue folder. Straightening, hands perched atop a chair, he spun his gaze right toward the pinboard and the six grisly photographs of the murdered man, James McNiff, pinned in a neat rectangle.

Half-drunk mugs of tea and coffee stood on the table before the officers. DC Bina Kaur sipped water and set the glass on the table.

'Morning everyone, sorry I'm late. Some plonker ran over a poodle at Harewood. Zero chance of a best in show at Crufts for the poor little soul this year, I'm afraid. How are we all this morning?'

Grumbled OKs and fines around the table.

'All the better for seeing you, boss,' Charlie Ings said in nasal estuary cockney.

'Thanks, Charlie. Feeling is mutual.' Wardell made his way

to the tea trolley. 'I see Mourinho lost it again at the post-match interview on Saturday, Charlie. You'll be playing in the Championship next season,' Wardell quipped.

Ings sniggered. 'Temporary blip. Mourinho will turn it around. Even the best of the best have bad days. You should know that.'

Wardell smirked, collected a mug, poured coffee from the pot, helped himself to a rich tea and turned to face the assembled detectives. 'Turn it around? Bad day? Five games without a win, Charlie. By Chelsea's standards, that's a catastrophe? Abramovich won't put up with results like that. Mark my words, he won't.'

'In The Special One we trust.'

'Don't make me laugh. You're sounding like a Gunner, Charlie. I'd watch out for that if I were you.'

'We'll never be as bad as the Gunners, boss. There's plenty more season left, yet.'

Wardell cast Ings a scathing look. 'For those of you who don't follow football, I'll interpret. What Charlie is trying to say is... Chelsea's pet Russian billionaire will gallop to the rescue, splash the cash and buy his way out of trouble with a couple of world class strikers. Hey presto, all will be well in the world.'

Mirthful sniggers echoed around the room.

'Cynical, but true,' Ings said. 'It's worked before and it'll work again. No point having billions if you don't splash it around every now and again, is there?'

Wardell shook his head, said, 'I suppose so...'

Setting the mug down, Wardell dragged out and lowered into a car. He breathed deep. Composed himself. Opened the blue folder. 'Time we got down to business. That's enough satire for one morning. I'm sure you all know why we're here. We're here to start the investigation into the murder of James McNiff. The murder happened between 10.00 a.m. and midday on Saturday

3rd January. Uniform found Mr McNiff deceased in his flat in Sandsend yesterday afternoon. Uniformed officers from Whitby forced entry and discovered him tied to a kitchen chair at 3.45 p.m. We're calling the investigation Stoker. For those of you unfamiliar with the relevance of classic horror to Whitby, I'll enlighten you. Much of Bram Stoker's novel, Dracula, is set in, and around, Whitby. Hence the relevance of Stoker. The photographs are from the locus. Our victim was shot twice in the forehead, and, his tongue removed. Yes, you heard right. Whoever killed him, cut out his tongue. Pathologist is of the opinion, the oral mutilation took place post mortem. The post mortem is scheduled for ten tomorrow morning. David, you and I will attend.'

'OK, boss,' Watts said, his nose crinkling into a grimace.

Wardell continued. 'It's important to note that we've yet to receive formal confirmation that Mr McNiff was indeed murdered. However, it's unlikely he shot himself twice in the head, then removed his own tongue. Would anyone care to disagree?'

Silence.

'No, thought not. We've yet to recover either the murder weapon, or the tongue. The killing shouts cold-blooded execution.' Wardell slurped coffee.

'I want everything passed to Marjorie. Marjorie's role is pivotal. She'll will control, organise and manage data input into the PNC. I don't want anyone, other than Marge, getting bogged down in admin. Is that understood?'

A chorus of enthusiastic affirmations rippled around the table.

'Good. If for any reason Marge is unavailable, Kelly will step into the breach. Happy, Kelly?'

'Over the moon, boss.'

'I assumed you would be,' Wardell said, grinning. 'Has

everyone read the letter I emailed yesterday? The letter written by, and handed to me personally, by McNiff, three days ago.'

Everyone nodded.

'It makes grim reading, boss,' Bina Kaur said.

'Dirty bastards abusing children like that,' Ings said. 'They ought to be strung up by their b–'

'I'm sure everyone shares your sentiments, Charlie, if not your vocabulary,' Wardell interjected, before Ings could finish his sentence.

'It's just...'

'We know, Charlie, we know... Mr McNiff made some very serious allegations, not only of abuse, but murder.'

'The bit about the baby, boss,' Ings said, 'it got to me.'

'In fairness, they're unproven allegations,' Watts said, directing his gaze at Wardell. 'Are *we* investigating the allegations of abuse, boss?'

Wardell nodded. 'Yes, David. I clarified that specific point with the Chief Super late yesterday. He okayed it. The allegations of abuse and murder will be one investigation. The fact is, twenty-four hours after depositing his statement with us, James McNiff is dead. To my mind, it's probable they're connected.'

'So, we work on that assumption?' asked Roberts, chewing on a biro.

'Yes, Kelly, until we establish otherwise. I'm going to request Billy Searle's post mortem is reviewed considering statements made by McNiff. He was adamant someone murdered Searle. Something may have got missed. There could be a link. Mind you, we ought not jump to conclusions. We must keep an open mind.'

The room fell silent.

DC Kelly Roberts broke the silence. 'Perhaps, we've got a contract killer on our hands, boss?' she said, with a glint in her eye. 'An assassin hired by the Church to clean up its dirty laundry before it gets into the public domain? The papers will have a field day, if they got hold of McNiff's statement.'

'You've been reading too much, Dan Brown, Kelly,' Ings said, mouth twisted into a scornful sneer. 'You ought to get out more.'

'Piss off, Charlie. Numpty.'

'Listen to her, MCU's very own tabloid journo. What a wonderful way with words you've got.'

Wardell slapped the table with the palm of his hand. 'Now, now, children, behave or I'll send you to your rooms without supper,' he said, glaring. 'Yes, the papers would, Kelly, *if* they were to find out. If anyone speaks to the press without my express permission, I'll suspend them. Is that clear?'

Everyone nodded. Roberts gave Ings the bird, turned to Wardell, nodded.

Wardell drew a breath. 'OK... If Searle *was* murdered and the same person killed McNiff, then they're building up a head of steam. It's imperative we hit the ground running. We need to locate the other alleged victims named in McNiff's statement, before the killer does.'

'Niall Daley and Colm Walsh, boss?' Kaur asked.

'That's right, Bina, Daley and Walsh. We need to find them, take statements and, if we consider it prudent, take them into protective custody. We need to create ourselves some breathing space. Given what we know already, I've grave concerns for the safety of both men.'

A contemplative silence dawned in the room. After a minute, from nowhere, David Watts released a huge wet fart which vibrated from the walls. A rotten egg stench filled the room.

'Ow!' exclaimed the others. Ings feigned to projectile vomit on the floor.

David Watts cupped his stomach in his hands. 'Sorry, boss. Everyone. Last night's bhuna. The damn thing keeps repeating on me. It's been giving me grief all morning. The last time I buy a curry from there.'

Wardell stalled, released the fingers clamping his nostrils together. 'I'd say so, David, I'd say so... OK, team, now is as good a time as any to break for coffee. Give David time to use the little boy's room. We'll reconvene in ten minutes. Everybody happy?'

Nods and yeses around the table.

When the meeting reconvened, Wardell divvied out tasks for Operation Stoker. Charlie Ings tasked to liaise with SOCO to recover the foetus. Bina Kaur to locate ex-soldier Colm Walsh. Kelly Roberts asked to locate and interview Niall Daley. Wardell and Watts would attend McNiff's post mortem and lead on the allegations of abuse. The priority being to interview Father O'Connell at his retirement home in York's leafy suburbs.

13

MONDAY 5TH JANUARY 2015, 8.30 A.M

Retired teacher John McAbe loved walking his dog, Blaze, along the muddy foreshore of the River Humber. He loved the solitude, the mental space and the physical connection with the sea. His morning constitutional added some much-needed structure to his day.

McAbe woke with the alarm at dawn, stumbled out of bed, got dressed, showered, and bounded downstairs. Wolfing down a bowl of porridge, he drained a cup of strong, black coffee. After feeding Blaze, the pair stepped outside into the birth of a freezing winter day.

Ten minutes later, man and dog arrived at the car park under the dunes.

Faces chapped by a chill east wind, nostrils charged with wet mud and salt, the pair raced over the dunes towards the river. As a slobbering Blaze strained on the lead, McAbe yanked on the thin strip of leather and brought the expectant dog to heel.

'Heel! Heel!' McAbe bellowed. 'Calm down, laddie. We'll be there soon enough.'

A whining Blaze sank onto his haunches and looked up at McAbe with sad eyes.

Man and dog started up the final dune and reached the summit. Below them lay the colossal mute brown snake of the River Humber. The river – bounded by an enormous expanse of mud – shimmered and sparkled in the low sun.

McAbe hunkered down, unclipped Blaze, whispered, 'Go on body, find a stick... Find a stick...'

Blaze bolted down the dune, arrived at the mud and scuttled forward, head down, tail up, sniffing the ground. Fifty yards distant, he slid to a halt, ears raised. Stiffening, he whined. McAbe followed Blaze's line of sight towards an indeterminate pile of detritus laid at the water's edge. A barking Blaze trotted towards the pile.

McAbe whistled. Blaze ignored his master's whistles. 'Daft wee bugger, come back!' McAbe slid down the dune sideways, and jogged towards Blaze, yelled, 'Come back!'

Blaze halted, sniffed the pile, collared neck twisting and turning, whines increasing to a growl.

A breathless McAbe arrived alongside Blaze. 'Sit, boy, *sit!*'

Blaze came to heel. The growls ebbed to silence. Blaze looked up with fear in his eyes, ears flattened along its neck.

A breathless McAbe inhaled lungfuls of air.

'Good boy,' McAbe said. 'What's up, lad, eh? What you found?'

McAbe clipped on the lead, stroked Blaze's ears and studied the curious pile through narrowed eyes. The pile measured two feet high, three feet wide and six feet long, composed of seaweed, driftwood and detritus. McAbe covered his brow against the sun's glare and saw something unusual. Squatting down, he reached over and parted a clump of seaweed. 'What the...'

McAbe reared upright, tightened his grip on the lead and dragged Blaze away across the sand. Blaze gagged and whined.

A solitary, lifeless human eye returned McAbe's gaze through a gap in the seaweed.

14

DC Kelly Roberts feathered the brakes of the seven-year-old metallic blue Citroen Picasso and brought the car to a halt behind the line of stationary vehicles. Selecting neutral, she put her head back against the rest and felt the tension uncoil in her arms, neck and shoulders.

The Clive Sullivan Way – the dual carriageway into Hull from the west – was a major pain in the backside. One minor accident and the entire dual carriageway would grind to a halt. Kelly couldn't recall ever having travelled it without getting into a jam. Two-foot-high orange dot matrix letters on the gantry advised, 'ACCIDENT.'

'Drive idiots! Drive!' Kelly cursed at no one in particular.

Exhaling a long sigh, she glanced into the mirror on the sun visor pulled down against the glare of the low sun and pushed strands of crimson hair from the centre of her forehead up to her hairline.

A long day had just got longer.

Checking the satnav, she confirmed that Niall Daley's place of work, The Bransholme public house, was still five miles distant. A cursory check of the Police National Computer suggested The Bransholme was a tough estate pub with a reputation for gang fights, after hours drinking and drugs busts. Two months prior, a Romanian drug dealer was killed in a knife fight in the car park. His body dumped in a skip at the back of the pub.

Kelly stared at the rear of the silver 3-Series Coupe BMW ahead. The driver waved his arms around. Kelly imagined him a jumped-up sales rep receiving a bollocking for not achieving target. Hoped it so. Cursing him under her breath, she allowed herself a wry smile. Reclaiming an e-cigarette from a door pocket, she sucked hard and the chemical concoction swirled inside her throat and raced to her brain. Although a poor substitute for the buzz of nicotine, it felt good.

As the road cleared, the traffic nudged forward. The BMW blasted ahead and took the exit at a speed well above the speed limit.

Cock! Any other day, my friend, you wouldn't have been so lucky.

Kelly's mobile – suckered to the windscreen – vibrated, then rang. THE GRINCH displayed on the tiny screen. Butterflies fluttering in the pit of her stomach, Kelly accepted the call.

'You arrived yet?' Wardell barked.

'No, boss. Traffic's dreadful. There was an accident. I've been stationary for ten minutes. Satnav is saying twenty minutes.'

'I see. Terrible road, that,' Wardell said, his tone softening. 'When you get there, use kid gloves. Find out if he's happy to provide a statement to corroborate McNiff's accusations. Don't press him too hard. Call me when you're through with him. Alright?'

'Yes, boss.'

'And, Kelly...'

'Boss?'

'Be careful. Hull's got its fair share of nutters. Organised

Crime reckon there's a massive synthetic marijuana problem in the city. A turf war between Romanian gangs. Give anyone who looks like a smack head a wide birth. OK?'

Kelly smirked. 'Don't worry, I will.' She stabbed the brakes, dragged left on the indicator. 'You know me, boss, I'm discretion personified.'

'Don't forget to call. I'll speak to you later.'

Wardell ended the call.

John Cleese's voice instructed Kelly to take the next left at the end of the slip road. Kelly smiled. John Cleese's company was the best seven fifty she had ever spent.

Negotiating two roundabouts, she slowed at a sign advising Bransholme a mile ahead. She drove past ranks of identikit sixties pre-fabs, tower blocks and shopping precincts.

Niall Daley worked at The Bransholme as an Assistant Chef, preparing two for a tenner meals six days a week, and a discounted carvery offer on Sundays. While not a sink estate, the area had a tired, deprived air. A massive estate redevelopment programme had been cancelled in the wake of the financial crash.

Rounding a corner, Kelly saw two middle-aged men in shiny turquoise shell suits and scuffed Adidas trainers. They sat on a low brick wall smoking hand roll-ups, bottles of cider on the pavement at their feet. Kelly sped past, focussed ahead.

Half a mile along, she turned left off the carriageway into the pub car park and pulled up next to a haphazard collection of timber smoking shelters defacing the mock Tudor frontage. She killed the engine, reached to the glove box and collected the post-it note with the manager's name. Buttoning up the jacket of her two-piece navy trouser suit, she reached for the door. Stepping out, two hoodies on BMXs skidded to a halt beside her.

'Ay up, missus, nice car. Give us a fiver, and we'll look after it. Smack heads round here will nick it in a heartbeat.'

Kelly stymied a wry smile. The spirit of free enterprise, it seemed, was alive and well in the council estates of west Hull.

'Shouldn't you two be at school?' Kelly asked, reaching for her purse.

'Inset day. No school today,' said the stick-thin, pock-faced youth. 'That's reight, innit, Tommo?'

'It is, argh. No school today or tomorrow. Are you going give us a fiver, or what?'

Kelly steered her eyes to the heavens. After thirty seconds, she returned her gaze to the youths and tried hard not to let her face betray amusement.

'I suppose I better had, hadn't I?' Kelly said, handing over two pound coins. 'If there's any damage, I'll hold you two responsible. I'll find you. Don't for one minute think I won't. You'll get the rest when I come back and there's no damage. OK?'

The youths nodded.

'Alright,' said the older one, stepping off his bike, laying it down on the tarmac and sitting on the kerb. 'How long will you be?'

'As long as it takes,' Kelly said, setting off for the entrance.

As Kelly stepped inside, a fug of stale beer and lemon cleaning fluid invaded her nostrils. Stalling, she gazed across an explosion of mahogany and burgundy dralon. Black and white photographs of Hull's Victorian fishing heydays hung on the walls. Fishing memorabilia cluttered almost every available surface. At her left shoulder, a bank of three fruit machines flashed and beeped. A freshly shaved mass of muscle in a wife-beater vest stood at a fruit machine, hoping for four cherries. In a corner, a group of old men in flat caps played dominoes. They glanced up as Kelly entered, then seeing nothing of interest, looked away and slurped on their pints. Sam Smith's latest adenoidal effort played low in the background. A waif-like teenage barmaid leaned on the back counter, studying her phone.

Kelly walked over, placed her hands on the bar and cleared her throat. The barmaid glanced up for less than a second, before returning her hollow gaze to the phone.

'Excuse me. Is the manager around?' Kelly said.

The barmaid exhaled a weary sigh without looking up.

'I said...'

The barmaid looked up. 'I heard. You a sales rep, or summat? Manager don't see reps without a prior appointment. You're wasting your time.'

Kelly stared daggers at the girl. 'No, I'm not selling anything. I'm a police officer.'

The barmaid dragged up from the counter, lay her mobile by the till.

Kelly displayed her warrant card. 'I'm Detective Constable Kelly Roberts of North Yorkshire Police. I'd like a word with the manager. I checked with head office. I'm told the manager's name is Mark Brown. Tell him someone wants to see him.'

'Alright... Keep your hair on. Wait here. Mark's upstairs doing the VAT return,' she said, turning and disappearing through a door in the back wall. 'I'll fetch him.'

'Thanks,' Kelly said, to the girl's back, lifting onto a stool.

The bar filled with the raucous clatter of an avalanche of coins.

'Get in!' exclaimed the man in the vest, sinking onto his haunches, cupping his hands around the coin outlet. 'You fucking beauty!'

Eventually, a door swung open. A Rottweiler in a white shirt and black slacks with a number one haircut appeared in the opening. Kelly aged him as in his early sixties. The teenage barmaid peered over the man's left shoulder. Settling a meaty, tattooed hand on the frame, he glanced over his shoulder. 'Thanks, Gemma, love. Have yourself a cuppa. I'll take over.' He looked past Kelly. 'It's not like we're busy, is it?'

Behind him, Gemma shrugged. 'No, I don't suppose we are,' she said, disappearing from view. The landlord stepped behind the bar, offered Kelly a drink on the house. Kelly declined.

'Gemma tells me you're a police officer. That right?'

'That's right, yeah. Name's Detective Constable Kelly Roberts. I work for North Yorkshire Police in the Major Crime Unit, based out of Harrogate.'

Brown's lips pursed and his eyebrows raised. Something approaching surprise overtook his expression. 'Major crimes, eh? Well, I never... Whatever's brought you here, it must be serious, since you've come so far. Is it about Saturday night? A WPC from Hull took a statement first thing Sunday morning. It was just a couple of lads letting off steam. I only called you lot, because they'd damaged the pool table. Insurers being what they are, they insist on a crime reference, otherwise I don't get a payout. You know what young'uns are like when they've had a skinful. It was innocent enough.'

'I'm not here about Saturday night, Mr Brown. I'd like a word, if I may, with one of your employees.'

'Which one? I've six full-time, and five part-time employees.'

'Niall Daley. Is he here? I'm told he works here as an assistant chef.'

'That's right, he does. Only, he's not here. He ought to be, but he isn't.'

'Did he call in sick?'

'No, he didn't. Truth is, I'm worried about him. Niall's one of my best workers. He's the quiet conscientious type; likeable with it. He's not one for taking unauthorised leave, isn't Niall. The thing is, I've not seen hide nor hare of him since his last shift on New Year's Eve. It's worrying. I've tried his mobile, but all I keep getting is the, *this number is unavailable*, pre-recorded message. To tell you the truth, I've given it up as a bad job. So far, he's missed three shifts, which is not like him. I'm planning to pop round to his flat later today, to see if everything's alright. The others can only cover his shifts for so long. Despite present appearances, we're busy most days.'

'Mm, I can imagine,' Kelly said. 'Do you have an address and a contact number for him?'

'Yes, love, I do. I'll nip upstairs and get it. It's upstairs in the filing cabinet. That's where I keep all the administrative bumf.'

'Please, if it's no trouble?'

'No, love, it's no trouble at all. And you're sure I can't get you a drink?'

'I'm fine, thanks. Once I've got his contact details, I'll be on my way.'

'Righto. Promise you'll let me know if you find him. Here, take my card. That's my mobile number.'

Brown gave Kelly a business card.

'When, and if I find him, I'll call you.'

'Make sure you do.'

Satisfied there was no damage to the car, Kelly paid the youths the three pounds owing. Settling into the driver's seat, she dialled Niall Daley's mobile and got the 'this number is unavailable' pre-recorded message. She dialled again, without success. After inputting Niall's postcode into the satnav, she waited and let it refresh. Niall's home showed as being just one and a quarter mile away.

Kelly turned left out of the car park and drove straight on for a mile. Passing through a street of 1970s semi bungalows, the satnav showed a left turn ahead. Kelly directed the nose of the car into a cul-de-sac of council-owned maisonettes.

Daley lived at Flat 5A, Filey Road. Kelly feathered the throttle, counted the numbers, slowed before 5A/5B and pulled into the kerb at a block of four maisonettes. She killed the engine, stepped out, locked the car and marched up the path toward the front door.

A pug-faced woman with a purple rinse in curlers leaned over the balcony above the front door. She reminded Kelly of Les Dawson's gossiping neighbour caricature. The woman's stare bore into the top of Kelly's skull. Kelly, addressing the footpath, hid her grin.

Reaching the door, Kelly looked up and said, 'Morning.'

'Morning, love,' said the woman, adding, 'Niall's not in. I haven't seen him since Thursday.'

'OK,' Kelly replied.

'Niall always lets me know if he's going off anywhere. It must've slipped his mind, I suppose.'

'He does, does he? Always?'

'Yes, love, *always*. Lovely man is Niall. He's a friend of mine.'

'And you're sure he's not at home? Thing is, I've travelled to see him.'

'I'm as sure as I can be, yes, love. The floors here are so thin, you can hear a pin drop downstairs. The last time I laid eyes on Niall was four days ago.'

'Thursday?'

'Aye, that's right, early Thursday morning. These days my memory is hopeless, but I remember it because I watched him climb into the back of a white van.'

'Was he alone?'

'No, love. He'd been talking with the driver. He got into the van and they drove off together,' she said. 'Anyway, love, I hope you don't mind me asking, but what's it got to do with you? You're asking an awful lot of questions.'

'I need to ask Niall a couple of questions, that's all, my darling. I'm a police officer.' Kelly flicked open her warrant card and held it aloft.

'Niall's not in trouble, is he?'

'Nothing like that, no. I'd like a quick word with him, that's all.'

'I see. Good. I wouldn't want him to be in any trouble.'

Kelly nodded. 'What did he look like?'

'Who, love?'

'The man Niall was speaking to Thursday morning.'

'Well, I remember he was slim and dressed smart. He was wearing a camel coat. It'll be before your time but it, the coat I mean, was just like the one Bernie Winters used to wear. And he had a lovely suntan. Brown as a berry, he was. You don't see his type around these parts very often. The type that looks like they've got a bob or two... Anyway, I've never seen him before, and I know most of Niall's friends. We look out for one another.'

'Do you remember the make and model of van he got into? It could be important.'

'No, love, sorry I don't. I'm useless with cars. I seem to remember it was white, small, and had stickers on the sides like rental vans do. If I remember right, it had a Leeds phone number. The area code for Leeds is 0 1 1 3, isn't it, my love?'

'Yes,' Kelly said, 'it is.'

'I thought it odd that Niall got into the back.'

'The back?'

'Yes, love, that's right. He climbed into the back. I thought it a little odd.'

'Why did you think it odd?'

'Because the passenger seat was empty, love, that's why. You'd expect someone to sit in the passenger seat if it was empty, wouldn't you? Maybe they were going to pick someone else up? Anyway, he, the tanned man, he shut the back doors, locked them, walked around to the driver's side, got in and drove off.'

Kelly nodded. 'Yeah, I suppose it seems a little odd, when you think about it. Do you mind if I pop upstairs and leave you a card with my contact details? I'd appreciate a phone call when Niall surfaces. As I say, I'd like a quick word with him.'

The woman nodded. 'No, not at all, my love. Pop up. I'll make us a nice cuppa. If you've the time, that is? You look like you could do with a hot drink.'

Why the hell not? thought Kelly. Updating an impatient Wardell could wait.

'By the way, love. If it's any help, I made a note of the van's registration number. I wrote it down on the calendar. You can't be too careful these days, can you?'

'I don't suppose you can. I'll be straight up,' Kelly said, smiling a wide smile.

15

MONDAY 5TH JANUARY 2015, 1.30 P.M

Wardell answered Kelly's call on the second ring. Pressing the phone tight against her ear, she heard a hubbub of voices in the background.

'How did you get on?' Wardell said. 'Don't keep me in suspenders.'

'There's good, and not so good news, boss,' Kelly said, erasing the image of Wardell wearing female lingerie. 'I called in at the pub where he works – The Bransholme.'

'Go on.'

'It's a bit of a dump, typical estate pub. The manager was helpful, though, hasn't seen or heard from Niall for three days.'

'OK. Have you tried raising him on his mobile? I take it he has one?'

'Yes, boss, he does. I tried, but all I'm getting is the, this number is unobtainable, message. The Bransholme's manager, he's been getting the same message for the last three days. Says he was planning on popping around to Niall's flat tonight. I left several messages asking him to return my call.'

'I see,' Wardell said. 'Text his number through. I'll have

Marge do some digging. Check his movements. Locate him via GPS. It may be premature, but it can't hurt... Is there anything else, Kelly?'

'Yes, boss. I went to Niall's home address. He lives in a ground floor maisonette: one of a block of four. The neighbour in the flat above watches out for him. She, too, told me he's not been home for three days. Boss, she saw him climb into the back of a white rental van early Thursday morning. She said he was speaking to the van driver before getting in. She didn't recognise him, but gave me a description: tanned, well-heeled. Boss, she's the gatekeeper type – all eyes and ears. In that cul-de-sac, nothing, would get past her.'

'OK. And?'

'And she thought it unusual, because the front passenger seat was empty.'

'So you think it's suspicious?'

'Yes, boss, I do. The neighbour says Niall always lets her know if he's going anywhere for any length of time. They look out for one another.'

'And the good news?'

'The neighbour took a note of the van's registration number.'

'She did?'

'Yes, boss, she did. It's CY12 OWN.'

'Excellent work. I'll have Marge perform VC and ANPR checks. Is there anything else? I'm sorry, but I've got to run. I'm seeing a man about a dog in ten minutes.'

'No, boss. That just about sums up my day.'

'OK. Well done. I'll see you when you get back. Drive careful.'

'I will,' Kelly said, but Wardell had already gone.

16

WEDNESDAY 10TH SEPTEMBER 1975, 11.30 P.M

Fuelled by anger and whisky, Colm halted on the wet grass under a stand of tall pines. He waited until his eyes had adjusted to the darkness. Twenty metres distant, he saw the dark outline of the ivy-clad gamekeeper's cottage. No light shone from the windows, no sounds disturbed the stillness of the night. He imagined Stan at the quiz night at The Feathers: third pint drunk, fourth lined up, arguing the toss with the resident know-it-all about the identity of the winning goal scorer in the 1935 FA Cup Final. Stan's absence would give him plenty of time to take the gun and return it to the cabinet afterwards.

Arriving at the door, he felt the icy burn of the key in his trouser pocket. Dragging it out, he looked down too quick. The keyhole blurred, swam and spun. Colm smashed his eyes closed and cast out a steadying hand onto the wall.

After a minute, composure regained, he took out a torch from his rucksack, switched it on and picked out the keyhole.

As the lock slid back, he stepped inside, dragged the door closed behind him and played the torchlight along the hallway, scouring the darkness. Satisfied nobody was home, he made his way to the kitchen. He turned on the light, switched the torch off, leaned against the worktop, gathering breath. Tracking his gaze left, he saw the gun cupboard, lifted from the worktop, padded over and opened it. He removed his favourite shotgun: a double-barrelled, Purdey 12-bore, stock lustrous in polished walnut, metalwork exquisitively etched with whorls and swirls. He weighed it in his hands. Loved it for itself. Checking the safety was engaged, he removed two cartridges from an ammunition box and locked the cabinet. Standing there, shotgun in his hands, he heard dry hinges creak, boots wiped across a mat and a raucous, phlegmy cough.

With the smooth precision borne of habit, he slipped two cartridges into the breach, cocked the long barrel, positioned the stock under his right armpit and flicked off the safety. With the barrel pointed to the floor, he settled his right index finger on the trigger.

If it was Stan, he could relax. Stan wouldn't do anything stupid with a gun around. He knew that much. He glared at the door, thrust out his chest, jaw set firm. Nothing would stop him now.

As the door creaked open, Stan swayed in the opening. Stalling, he rocked on his heels, regained his balance. His uncertain frown twisted into a scowl of confusion. He brought with him a waft of real ale, spirits, and glazed eyes. Eyelids batting, he seemed not to see Colm. Scowl evaporating, a blend of surprise and uncertainty dawned on Stan's lean and craggy face.

'Ay up, lad. You made me jump. What the bloody hell you doing in here?' Stan exclaimed, gaze fixed on the shotgun. 'And the gun? What are you doing with that gun?'

'This?'

'Aye, that! Don't be a clever bugger, lad. It doesn't suit!'

'I'm going shooting. You told me I could use the gun whenever I liked.'

'I did... But...'

'But nothing, Stan. What's it got to do with you anyway?'

Anger flared behind Stan's eyes. 'I'll tell thee what it's got to do with me, shall I? That's my gun you've got slung under your bloody armpit. It's my responsibility, as well, you know. Anyway, you ought to be tucked up in bed at this late hour. Did you shit the bed or summat?'

'I couldn't sleep. I've got a lot on my mind.'

'Oh, you have, have you?' Stan said, leaning on the door frame. 'Bugger this for a game of soldiers. It's time I took the weight off my feet. It's been a long day...'

Stan wobbled to the table, dragged out a chair and slumped into it. Exhaling an exasperated sigh, he gazed at the tea-ring stained pine and hiccupped. Colm rounded the table and stood over Stan.

Stan looked up. 'What you thinking of shooting, Anyway?'

Colm shrugged. 'Crows. Pigeons. Bag myself some rabbits. Anything. I'm not fussed. I'm in the mood to kill something. There's plenty of vermin around here.' Colm said, blinking, words spooling from his mouth like ticker tape at a homecoming parade, gaze shifting to the school.

Stan sensed something serious in the offing. Colm's usual cheery innocence, absent. His eyes widened. 'Usually, you let me know in good time when you want to borrow the gun.' He burped. 'Excuse me, pig, I am. That new ale they've got on down at The Feathers, keeps repeating on me, sodding Lancashire shite. Christ knows why Terry's stocking it. I expect bugger's getting a kick-back from the brewery, or summat. Colm, why don't you sit down? We'll have ourselves a chat.' Stan dragged out a chair, gestured for Colm to sit. 'Get whatever's bothering you off your chest.'

'I'd rather stand, thanks.'

'Have it your own way, lad,' Stan said. 'If there's owt I can do to help, you know you can talk to me, don't you? Bottling things up never did anyone any good.'

Colm shook his head. 'Nothing's up, Stan. I'm fine. Honest, I am. It's just this place... It pisses me off.' A shallow nod towards the school. 'The priests and the nuns are evil. I hate them. I could...' Colm noticed Stan's gaze fix on the shotgun. 'What's up, Stan? Don't you trust me?'

Stan reached over his shoulder, collected a bottle of twelve-year-old malt from the dresser, spun off the lid, poured three fat fingers into a tumbler and sank half.

'It's not about trust, lad,' Stan said, weather-beaten face etched with concern. 'I don't know... Only... You seem edgy... If I'm not mistaken, that's alcohol I can smell on your breath. Have you been drinking, lad?'

Colm shrugged.

'I'm not used to seeing you like this, that's all. You sure you're alright? I've never known you like this. You can talk to me, you know. A while back, you mentioned a lass, then you clammed up. You never said another word about her. Colm, put the gun down, take the weight off your feet and I'll treat you to a snifter of this fine malt. It's no fun drinking alone. The vermin can wait.'

Colm shook his head. The vertical crease above his eyes deepened. The fire in his eyes burned a little brighter. 'No, thanks, Stan.' Colm paused, a thin smile flitted across his lips. 'Look, I'm getting off,' he said, stepping to the door. 'I've vermin to see to. The decision's made.'

As Colm came past, Stan grasped his arm. Their eyes met.

'Now, you listen here, lad, and listen good. Don't do owt daft. I've heard rumours. Tales of terrible goings on. Tittle tattle. It's none of my business what goes on inside that school, I keep my head down and my nose clean. I do my job. All I'm saying is... Don't do owt stupid. Something you'll regret for the rest of your life. Whatever's mithering you, lad, take my advice ... let it go.

You've got your entire life ahead of you. You know that, don't you? It'd be a crying shame to waste it.'

Colm struggled free of Stan's grip and bolted to the door.

At the door, he spun to Stan. 'Don't worry, I won't do anything daft. If anyone asks, you've not seen me, and I've not seen you. Thanks for caring, Stan. I'm getting off. Don't worry, I'll put the gun back. Enjoy the whisky.'

Stan shrugged, nodded. 'Alright lad, have it your own way. Anyone asks, I've not seen you,' he said. 'And you've not seen me...'

'That's right, Stan,' Colm shouted from the doorstep. 'We've not seen one another.'

Stan switched off the electric blanket, rolled into bed, dragged under the sheets and savoured the warmth. Above him, the room gyrated and swam. Closing his eyes, he saw swirling grey worms against a black felt background.

Balanced on the edge of sleep, he heard the dull boom of a shotgun discharging. His eyes quivered open. In the gloom, he saw the familiar outline of the roof structure. Raising on an elbow, he listened hard, but heard only silence.

Shrugging, concluding that the sound was a nightmare brought on by drink, he rolled onto his side and closed his eyes.

On the edge of sleep, he heard distant, raised voices, a dull boom and a scream. Then, nothing, as silence reclaimed the night.

17

MONDAY 5TH JANUARY 2015, 5.00 P.M

Wardell settled a mug on the tea-stained coaster. Only himself and Charlie Ings were in the office. Everybody else, either tasked on duties, which had taken them out of the office, or away from their desks. He signed the last timesheet and added it to the pile. Pushing back from the desk, rubbing his eyes, he sat back and exhaled a weary sigh.

Wardell's landline trilled. 'Wardell,' he rasped.

'Alan, it's Amanda. Are you OK? You sound fed up.'

'Oh, hello, Amanda,' Wardell said, tone brightening. 'I've just spent two hours sorting time sheets. It's not my idea of fun. Anyway, less of my troubles. How's life treating you this fine day?'

'I can't complain. Alan, I'm calling about Billy Searle.'

'Searle?'

'Suicide? Masham? Last week? You asked me to call in on the pathologist, Taylor, in York. Ring any bells?'

Wardell pressed the phone tight against his ear, interest and curiosity aroused. 'Sorry, yes. *That* Billy. I'm with you now. For a second, my mind went blank. It must be the sodding timesheets. My brain, it's atrophied. How did you get on?'

'He took some persuading. I almost had to beg to get an audience. He agreed, eventually and took me through the post mortem, line-by-painful-line. He made it perfectly obvious he wasn't happy to see me.'

'No, I don't suppose he would have been. He's a useless bugger, at the best of times. He ought to have been put out to grass years back. You stepping into his shoes can't come quick enough.'

'That's as may be... Are you sitting comfortably, Alan?'

'I am,' Wardell said. 'Why? What's up?'

'Alan, it's very unlikely Billy Searle committed suicide. The evidence indicates someone garrotted him while he was seated. Post mortem, someone strung him up. Alan, someone tried very hard to conceal a murder.'

'I see. You're sure about that?'

'Yes. His neck wounds are much more horizontal than the inverted v-shaped bruises characteristic of suicide by hanging. There's a marked difference between the two. I asked a friend of mine for a second opinion. He's a pathologist with over forty years' experience – a chap called Thomas Johansson. He works for the Met. Have you heard of him, Alan?'

'Sorry, I can't say that I have, no.'

'I sent him photographs and video. He got back to me five minutes ago. He agrees with my conclusion.' Wardell heard the closing sequence of a laptop. 'I'm sorry, Alan, but I've got to go. Are we still on for tonight?'

Wardell's concentrated frown relaxed. 'Yes. If you are?'

'I am.'

'Did you organise a sitter?'

'I did. Same girl as last time. She's sleeping over. Amazing what the promise of an extra tenner will do. I'll have to leave first thing. The sitter needs to be at college at half eight.'

'So long as you don't wake me up when you leave. They don't call me The Grinch around these parts for nothing.'

'I'll try my best not to disturb you.'

'You do that. I'll see you later. How does half six at my place sound?'

'Sounds perfect. Bye, for now, Alan.'

'Oh, one other thing before you go...'

'Yes, Alan?'

'Thanks,' Wardell said. 'When can I expect the revised post mortem?'

'Doctor Taylor mentioned late Friday. I asked his secretary to contact you direct. Is that alright?'

'That's fine by me, yes.'

'Good. That's sorted then.'

'I'll see you later. Drive careful.'

'You will. Ciao, Alan.'

'Yeah, ciao,' Wardell said, trying to sound hip.

18

TUESDAY 6TH JANUARY 2015, 8.30 A.M

DC Charlie Ings drifted the ten-year-old black Audi A4 towards the imposing oak front door of St Aubert's School for Boys. He pulled into a parking bay, killed the engine and dragged the seat back on its runners. Cranking the backrest to a near horizontal recline, he lay back, closed his eyes, drew a weary breath and expelled a long, exasperated sigh. Behind his eyes, an inch-high elf operated a jigger pick with gusto.

The drive from Leeds was uneventful. He had made good time. Arriving half an hour early, he decided on a nap before the expected arrival of the SOCO team and council workmen.

Yet still, dark thoughts rampaged through his mind.

Twenty-four hours earlier, Wardell notified Charlie that his promotion to Detective Sergeant had been put, once again, on the back burner. Wardell had cited funding issues.

Yes, boss... Whatever... Same shit, different day, thought Charlie.

To add insult to injury, Chelsea's rapid fall from grace was fast becoming a weeping sore. Mid-table, mid-season: *what was all that about?* Weren't the Blues meant to be one of Europe's top clubs?

He didn't need his ex-wife's vitriolic threats, either. The future of his six-year old son's Wednesday night sleepovers hung in the balance. Was there a soul inside that ice-cold exterior? Why did she hate him? Hadn't she been the one who'd done the dirty? Their telephone conversation had been short, loud and acrimonious. He had called her a whore and slammed the phone down so hard the cradle had split. Fuming, he had downed a quart bottle of Glenfiddich like a Buckfast-charged Glaswegian at a free bar. Now, the morning after, he regretted the whisky and swore at the little bastard working the jigger pick behind his forehead.

Charlie dragged up on the steering wheel, fumbled in the door pocket and recovered a foil pack of paracetamol. Releasing two, he swallowed them with water and lay back. Five minutes and the elf wielding the jigger pick took a tea break, and he dissolved into a fitful sleep.

Tap. Tap. Tap.

Charlie juddered awake. A toothy grin appeared through the condensation on the door glass. He reached for the switch. The glass whirled into the door.

'Morning, Charlie. Catching up on your beauty sleep, I see?'

Charlie chuckled. 'Droll, Kenny, very droll. Keep it down, mate. I've a bastard of a headache. Thought I'd catch myself forty winks.' Charlie looked past Chief SOCO Kenny Goddard towards a white van. 'I see your lot are champing at the bit?' he said, nodding toward the van bearing the council crest. 'Nice to see the council arrived on time.'

Goddard nodded. 'We're raring to go. We're all yours. Any chance you could wangle a brew? It's brass monkeys this morning.'

Charlie grinned. 'I'll try my best. Priests and nuns run this place. There's more chance of bread and wine.'

'You know me, Charlie, I'm not fussy. A nice Rioja to warm the cockles would go down a treat.'

Stepping out of the Audi, Charlie trudged to the front door. Before he had the chance to knock, the door creaked open. A squat, elderly nun stood on the threshold. She wore a brown habit and white veil. A pair of shiny black toe caps protruded under the hem of her habit. Folding her arms under her bosom, her wrinkled face creased into a sour pout.

'Are you from the police?' she snapped.

'Yes, that's right, Sister.' Charlie held up his warrant card. 'I'm Detective Constable Charlie Ings of North Yorkshire Police Major Crime Unit. I've an appointment with Father Thomas O'Malley at nine. We spoke yesterday on the phone.'

'We've been expecting you. I'm Sister Bernadette,' the nun said, spinning on heels. 'Follow me. Father O'Malley's upstairs, in his study.'

The nun spoke at a rate of knots Ings found difficult to comprehend.

Charlie followed Sister Bernadette along an oak panelled corridor past gilt-framed portraits of priests and sign-written boards with the names and attendance dates of notable former pupils. He followed the nun up an impressive staircase onto the first floor landing. Sister Bernadette halted, spun to him, pointed to a panelled door at the end of the landing, just visible in the gloom.

'Last door on the left. Knock once and wait. Don't keep rapping like an eejit,' she said. 'The Father will see fit to answer when he's good and ready.'

Sister Bernadette negotiated past Charlie and bounded downstairs without uttering another word.

Charlie marched along the corridor, knocked, stood and waited.

Several minutes passed without reply.

Peeved, he rapped loudly on the door and mumbled a profanity under his breath. So much for his nine o'clock appointment. Charlie hated tardy timekeeping. He settled his hand on the knob, reconsidered, and removed his hand. Stepping back, he leaned on the wall and stared at the door.

Five further minutes passed.

'Enter,' boomed a curt voice.

Startled, Charlie jumped.

Charlie passed through the door into a large room bathed in sunlight. A man sat behind a desk silhouetted by the sun. A chimney breast jutted from the wall on the left. In the alcove by the window, right of the chimney breast, an oak sideboard. Central upon the sideboard stood a carved mahogany statue of the crucifixion. To the right of the desk, an emerald green leather sofa faced a television.

The silhouetted man rose and moved out from the glare. The priest folded his arms across his chest and studied Charlie with circumspection. He was a short, slightly built man, with jet black curly hair and a gaunt weasel face.

'Good morning, Father. We spoke yesterday, on the phone,' Charlie said, proffering a hand.

The priest studied Charlie's outstretched hand, but made no move to shake it. His arms stayed folded across his chest. 'Might I see your identification?' O'Malley said, in the thickest of Dublin brogues.

'Here you go,' Charlie said, extracting his warrant card from a breast pocket. Accepting the card, the priest pulled it to within an inch of his face. He studied it, thrust it back.

'You can't be too careful. Lots of charlatans about, nowadays.'

'I can assure you, Father, I am who I say I am. Phone my superior officer, DI Wardell, if you like. He'll vouch for me.'

O'Malley shook his head, shrugged, gave Charlie an indifferent, superior look. 'There will be no need for that. What, might I ask, does this concern, DC Ings? You were a tad cagey on the telephone.'

'I was?' Charlie said. 'I'm sorry if you thought that, Father. I didn't mean to be. The reason I'm here is, *sensitive.*'

'I see,' O'Malley spun on a heel, returned behind the desk. 'Please, DC Ings, take a seat. Can I get you something to drink? A tea? Or perhaps a coffee?'

'Not at the moment, thank you.'

Charlie sat. They exchanged polite smiles across the desk. A pregnant pause settled in the space between them.

O'Malley spoke first: 'So, tell me... This reason for your visit, it is, in your own words, sensitive. In what way is it considered sensitive?'

'I'm sorry, Father, I'm not at liberty to divulge that.' Ings stalled, softened his tone. 'Father, may I ask you a question?'

'You may.'

'Do you know Father Flynn O'Connell? I understand he was your predecessor, here?'

'Flynn O'Connell... Flynn O'Connell... No, I can't say that I know him personally. Of course, I know him by reputation. As you say, Father O'Connell was my predecessor. He was the headmaster for fifteen years between 1975 and 1990. I'm told he did a grand job. That, he put St Aubert's on the map academically. Father O'Connell still owns a holiday cottage in the school grounds. He's a private man, likes to keep himself to himself. So far, I've not had the privilege of meeting him.' O'Malley's eyes darted past Charlie's left shoulder. 'Turn around, Detective Ings, that portrait on the wall behind you, is Father O'Connell. It's dated 1982. We're sat in what was his study.'

Charlie glanced over his shoulder, saw a portrait of a seated priest, The Holy Bible pressed against his chest.

Charlie looked to O'Malley. 'You say this was Father O'Connell's study?'

'Yes, that's right. Is it relevant?'

Charlie, recollecting McNiff's statement, glanced right to the leather sofa: imagined the depravity. Imagined too, what lay under the floorboards beneath the sideboard only feet from where he sat. Trying hard to expunge the images from his head, he returned his gaze to the priest.

'Look out of the window, Father.'

'Why?'

'Father, please, humour me.'

A flame of annoyance ignited in O'Malley's eyes. He glanced over his shoulder. Saw the SOCO van and two council workmen leaning on the bonnet of the council liveried van, next to it.

'I see you've brought the cavalry. Might I ask why?' O'Malley said.

'With good reason, father. Someone, a reliable source, suggested we search the floor void under the floorboards in the alcove beside the chimney breast,' Charlie said, rolling his eyes left. 'My job is to lift the floorboards, inspect, and recover anything we find. If we find anything, we'll secure the room. Father, I'd ask for your help in this matter. I can assure you, we'll reinstate everything to your entire satisfaction.'

O'Malley's expression puckered into a thoughtful frown. He fell silent. A minute passed. 'I take it you've brought along a valid search warrant? Without one I cannot, under any circumstances, allow your men access. The Bishop in Leeds must give his express permission for any intrusive search of any property. I'm sorry, DC Ings, but that's the way it is.'

Charlie grinned. 'Yes, Father, we came prepared. I have a warrant.'

Charlie handed the search warrant to O'Malley. O'Malley put on a pair of reading glasses. Studied the warrant. Handed it back to Charlie.

'When would you like to start?'

'Straight away, Father. There's no time like the present.'

19

TUESDAY 6TH JANUARY 2015, 9.30 A.M

A beaming Ings stepped outside and gave Goddard and the council workmen the thumbs up. A workman sidled over, perched on the Audi's bonnet.

'Are we good to go?'

'Damn right we are. The search warrant did the trick. Amazes me how a piece of paper can oil the wheels.'

'We'll get our gear sorted, then. Name's Terry. Mucker's name is Malcolm.'

They shook hands.

'Gaffer said something about lifting and re-fixing floor-boards?' Terry said. 'That right?'

'Yes. That's right. Don't worry, it isn't a big area. A sideboard needs moving first. It looks heavy to me.'

'We're not likely to find owt grisly, are we? Only, I treated myself to a full English this morning, and I'd like to keep hold of it, if you catch my drift.'

Ings smirked. 'Your breakfast's safe. Whatever's hidden in the floor we're told is in an old Quality Street tin,' Charlie said. 'You need to remove enough of floorboards so we can get at it. Once you've done that, nip off for a brew, give it an hour and come back and screw them back down. We'll do the rest.'

'Fine by me, mate,' Terry said, heading off to the van, whistling The Match of The Day theme tune.

Kenny Goddard watched Charlie approach, stepped down from the van, stretched and groaned. 'There's nothing better than a good stretch to get the blood flowing. We've not had a wasted journey, have we, Charlie? Did the man in black give you any grief?'

'Not as you'd notice, no. We've got the green light. As you might expect, the warrant did the trick. Here's hoping we've not had a wasted journey.'

'Were the natives restless?'

'A smidgeon, yes. Nothing I couldn't handle, though.'

'Good. We'll get suited up then.'

'You do that, Kenny.'

* * *

The council workmen removed a metre wide, two metre long section of floorboards in less than an hour.

Malcolm helped Terry to his feet. 'Reckon, that's it?' Terry said, pointing to a ten-inch diameter, dusty metal disc wedged between the joists.

Ings sank onto his haunches, studied the disc, nodded. 'Looks about the right size,' he said, turning to Goddard. 'Kenny, any chance you could wipe some dust off? Our witness said we'd find a Quality Street tin.'

Goddard snapped on a pair of rubber gloves, reset the cotton face mask over his nose and mouth, and pulled on the hood. Crouching down, he wiped way an inch-wide layer of dust from the disc. A faded 1970s vintage Quality Street logo emerged from the dust. Kenny caught a cough behind a fist. 'Happy, Charlie?'

'As a pig in shit, Kenny, as a pig in shit.'

20

TUESDAY 6TH JANUARY 2015, 3.00 P.M

PCs Martin Freeman and Danny Ashton sat warming their hands on the blast of hot air from the panda car heater. A trawler drifted into view halfway to the horizon, chased by a squadron of squawking seagulls. Its heading suggested Whitby as its ultimate destination.

'I don't know about you, Danny, but I'm frozen to the marrow. I can't feel my toes. Sod this for a game of soldiers. Door-to-door in the middle of winter, it isn't my idea of fun,' moaned Freeman.

'Nor mine,' Ashton sniffled, wiping a bulb of snot from under his nostrils with a sleeve. 'Anyway, how did you get on? Turn up anything?'

'Nothing of any interest, no,' Freeman replied. 'Waste of bloody time, if you ask me. Nobody's seen or heard, a thing. You?'

Ashton gazed, dead-eyed, out to sea.

'Well?'

'Sorry, Martin. I reckon I have.'

'Did what?'

'Turn up something. The old biddy two doors up, she reckons she saw McNiff early Saturday morning.'

'Oh, aye, where?'

'She said she saw McNiff climb into the back of a white rental van, near to the flat. Asked whether there was any truth in the rumours he'd had his tongue cut out. I dodged the question. Told her, no. It was obvious she didn't believe me. She gave me the evil eye. As I was leaving, she wished McNiff good riddance. Said he got on her nerves. That he used to play heavy metal into the early hours. Says she and him didn't get on. That they'd argued about the music and the powerful aroma of skunk coming from his flat. She might be old, but she's no dingbat,' Ashton said, blowing warm breath through joined hands. 'She's a rum bugger. I hope I've got a brain like hers when I'm that old.'

'Well, well, what a tosser. Selfish sod got what was he deserved then, didn't he? I can't stand folk like that.'

'Bit harsh that Martin, don't you think? Seeing as someone butchered the poor bastard.'

'No, I bloody well don't think it's harsh. I can't stand people like that. Going through life inflicting their fucked-up life choices on everyone else.'

A minute passed in a strained silence.

'And she sure it was McNiff she saw?' Freeman asked.

'She sounded confident enough to me,' Ashton replied.

'Did she note the registration?'

'No. She recognised the make and model, though.'

'And?'

'It was a white Ford Transit Connect, identical to the one her eldest son drives.'

'That's something, then. Better than nowt.'

'Ought to keep the Sarge happy.'

'Let's hope so.'

Danny Ashton dragged the seatbelt on. 'Let's call it a day.

Get back to the ranch. Have a brew. We've done our bit for Queen and country, and the good people of North Yorkshire today.'

'Sound like a plan,' Freeman said, inserting the key in the ignition with a relieved grin.

21

TUESDAY 6TH JANUARY 2015, 10.15 A.M

Detective Constable Bina Kaur studied her reflection in the vanity mirror. Inches above her head, rain did a fragile dance on the mohair hood. Lifting her chin, she checked her make-up in the sun visor mirror, refreshed her lipstick and flashed blusher along strong cheek bones. She steered her gaze to the dashboard clock. It read 10.15 a.m.; already fifteen minutes late.

Bina had called ahead and informed Colonel Tom Woolverton she expected to be late. He'd agreed to give her another half an hour. Mumbled something about pressing commitments.

It took two circuits of the car park before she found a parking space. Relieved, she applied the handbrake and killed the engine. Reaching into the rear, she dragged a knee-length black cashmere overcoat forward between the front seats, stepped out of the car and put it on.

Racing across the car park, shielding her long black mane from the worst of the rain, she slid to a halt under the guard room canopy beside the rifle-toting guard. He swung and held the door open. Stepping inside, she brushed raindrops from the fine cashmere and smiled at the guard.

'Thanks. Brrr. This weather is the worst. I detest winter,' Bina said, glancing toward the long queues snaking to the counter.

'You're welcome,' the guard said, nodding. 'Rain's set in for the day, I reckon.' Bina recognised the guard's West Country burr.

Behind a counter, at the head of the queues, civilian staff in white shirts with black and red stitched logos, manned computer terminals.

'Is it always this busy?' Bina asked.

'Most mornings, yes. It'll quieten down after lunch.'

'I see,' Bina smiled, flashed her warrant card. 'I'm here on important police business. Can I have a quiet word, please,' she whispered.

The guard nodded. 'You can, my darling. This way.'

They stepped into a quiet corner, away from the queues. The guard said: 'How can I help?'

'I'm Detective Constable Bina Kaur of North Yorkshire Police Major Crime Unit. I'm meeting Colonel Tom Woolverton at ten in the NAAFI. He knows I'm running late. The thing is, the Colonel, he can only spare me half an hour. He's got another meeting at eleven. I need to see him, today. My visit is in connection with a murder inquiry. As you might imagine, time's of the essence.' Bina flicked a gaze at the queues. 'If I have to queue...'

The penny dropped with the guard. 'OK. Follow me. Keep your head down. Try not to make eye contact.'

'Thank you so much.'

Bina heard grumbles of dissent as they walked past. At the counter, she stood within touching distance of the guard and feigned to study her phone. After a brief conversation, one of the counter staff handed a pink 'DAY VISITOR' badge to the guard.

'Here. Clip this on. This time – since you're in a hurry – I've vouched for you. This once, mind. Sign in. Follow me.'

Formalities completed, they stepped away from the counter, passed outside through double doors and halted under a canopy. The guard pointed to a single-storey building in yellow brick.

'That's the NAAFI. A word of warning. Give the coffee a miss. It's terrible. They use powdered stuff. Tea's terrible, too. Good news is, the hot chocolate is to die for. If I were you, stick to that.'

Bina nodded, smiled. 'Thanks. I'll remember that,' she said. 'And thanks for helping me jump the queue. Appreciated.'

The guard grinned. 'You're welcome. If you're ever at a loose end in Catterick on a Friday or Saturday night, give The Dog and Gun a go. It's my local. Most weekends, a good crowd comes in. I promise, you won't regret it.'

'I'll bear that in mind. Sounds like fun. Thanks again.'

'I'll see you around.'

'Yeah, you just might,' Bina said, eyes rolling, setting off towards the *NAAFI.*

Men, she thought, *are irrepressible.*

Stepping into the dining hall, a hundred enquiring male eyes met hers, and discernible lull in the conversation followed. Ignoring the unwanted attention, Bina scanned the hall. Over by the window, a soldier in combats waved. She weaved through and around tables and chairs.

Colonel Tom Woolverton was much as Bina had imagined. Early forties, lean, muscular, and ruggedly handsome. He wore combats and a khaki green t-shirt – taut across huge pecs. A simple silver crucifix hung around his neck. A five-inch long Action Man scar diagonally across the left side of his forehead.

'DC Bina Kaur?'

Bina nodded. 'That's right. Sorry, I'm late. Sod's law being what it is, I got caught in traffic.'

'Yes, well, now that you're here... I'm very pleased to meet you,' Woolverton said. They shook hands. 'Please, take a seat. Can I get you something to drink?'

Bina shook her head. 'Not for me, thanks. Since you're pushed for time, we'd better crack on.'

'If you wouldn't mind. I'm sorry about that, only, my eleven o'clock is rather important. I can't dodge it. I understand you'd like to discuss Colm Walsh. Is that right?'

'It is. Thanks for meeting me,' Bina said, shuffling out of her overcoat, placing it on the back of the chair. 'Phew. That's better. I was boiling over.'

Bina sat.

'So, tell me, what's this about? I admit to being a little anxious when you said you were with the Major Crime Unit. Colm isn't in trouble, is he? Before I forget, this is the latest photograph we have of him.'

Woolverton handed Bina a head and shoulders mugshot, creased along the middle.

'Thanks,' Bina said, accepting the photograph. 'Not that we know of, no. We need to speak to him. Colonel, one of Colm's closest school friends was murdered, recently. Two days prior, the victim came to us with a written statement setting out allegations of abuse. They were serious allegations. The victim named Colm in his statement. As you might imagine, we're very keen to establish Colm's current whereabouts. We need to interview him, take a statement.'

'Abuse, eh, that's dreadful. Of the sexual kind, I imagine?'

Bina glanced around, nodded. 'In confidence, yes, they are.'

'Almost every day it seems someone's on the news claiming they're the victim of sexual abuse. After a while, sad though it may be, you become inured to it.'

'I know what you mean,' Bina said. 'Colonel, how well did you know Colm Walsh?'

Woolverton shrugged. 'As well as any commanding officer knows any of the soldiers under his command, I suppose. It's an essential part of the job to maintain a professional distance between the men under one's command. I commanded Colm for three tours of Afghan. He was a dependable, conscientious, an effective soldier in all key respects. Colm was fearless in a fire-fight. A credit to the regiment. During his time here, he received two medals for gallantry. Before he joined The Yorkshire Regiment, he was with The Anglians. He came to us with an impeccable service record. I tried, though failed, to get him to change his mind about him leaving the army. It was a terrible shame. The army needs men like Colm Walsh. At the moment, there's a lot of what you civvies call churn. Very few people give the army a fair crack of the whip. It's a sad fact, career soldiers are rapidly becoming a thing of the past.'

'Have you kept in touch with Colm since he left the army, Colonel? He seems to have fallen off the radar.'

'After you called, I asked around. The last contact anyone has had with him was a text message received two months ago. The message was brief. I seem to recall it said he was staying in a homeless hostel very near York Minster. He didn't give an address. It's a sad reflection on society when heroes like Colm have nowhere to call home. Adapting to civilian life is difficult enough without the added trauma of not having a roof over one's head. The Americans take good care of their veterans. They've learned the hard way from the mistakes they made post Vietnam. It's long overdue that we do the same.'

'A text message, you say?'

'Yes. Unfortunately, the squaddie who received lost his phone. So I'm afraid there's no chance of a number.' Woolverton glanced at his watch. 'I'm very sorry, DC Kaur, but I really must be on my way. We've a NATO exercise in the wilds of Norway in the offing. Since Putin started flexing his muscles, we've moved to a higher state of combat readiness. I've all manner of things to organise. Anything else I can help you with?'

Bina nodded. 'No, you've been very helpful. Thank you for your time, Colonel. It seems a tour of the homeless hostels of York beckons.'

'There are worse places: Afghan for one, Iraq for another. I could make a list. The army takes you to some desperate shitholes. I'm sorry I couldn't have been more helpful. If you've time, get a drink and a bite to eat at the counter, on me. Leave my name at the till.'

'Thanks, I will. I'm feeling rather peckish.'

'A word of warning. Steer clear of the coffee. It's like bloody dishwater.'

22

TUESDAY 6TH JANUARY 2015, 12.15 P.M

Ings took a final drag on the cigarette and launched the butt across the wet gravel. In his peripheral vision, he glimpsed a lanky figure approaching in double tweed and a deerstalker. A broken shotgun hung over the man's right forearm; a brace of dead rabbits, feet tied with string, limp over his left shoulder.

'Afternoon.' A shallow dip of the head. 'If I were thee, I'd clean that up afore anyone sees it.'

'You would, would you?'

'Aye, I would. The priests and nuns that run this place see it, they'll have you in the confessional as quick as you can say, I repent my sins. They can be mean buggers when they want to be.'

'Sorry,' Ings said, stepping out from the entrance canopy, extinguishing the cigarette butt with a heel, picking it up. Rising, Ings caught a whiff of spirits on the breeze. He faced the man. 'It's a disgusting habit, anyway. I ought to stop. Is there a bin, nearby? There's never one around when you need one.'

'Give it here, lad. I'll see to it.'

'You don't have to.'

'It's no trouble,' the man said, arm outstretched, palm upturned. 'It's no trouble at all. By the way, lad, name's Stan Oldroyd. I'm the gamekeeper here. And who may I ask are you?'

Depositing the butt in Stan's palm, Ings introduced himself. Despite it being only a few minutes past midday, Stan reeked of whisky. Ings thought him three sheets to the wind already.

Ings said: 'A school with a gamekeeper, that's unusual.'

'Aye, I expect it is. School's the biggest landowner around here. Owns near to a hundred acres, it does. There's plenty of work needs doing. Anyway, what's going on?' Stan said, raising his chin toward the scenes of crime and council vans. 'Is there trouble at t'mill?'

Charlie grinned. The directness and dry humour of Yorkshire folk never failed to amuse him.

'There might be,' Ings shrugged.

'There might be? What kind of answer it that, lad? Either there *is*, or there *isn't*. What do you take me for, lad, an idiot? There's nowt gets past me round here. I've worked here for best part of forty years. I know this place, inside out, back to front.'

Stan swayed on his heels, almost losing his footing. Ings reached out and placed a steadying hand on Stan's forearm. Stan regained his balance.

'You alright?' Ings queried. 'You almost keeled over.'

'I'm fine, lad. Perhaps, a little unsteady on my feet, but I'll be alright. I expect I've overdone it on the malt. I can't seem to shift this bloody cold. I must have had it for going on for a month now. Terrible, it is. Hanging on like a bloody leech. Nowt'll shift it. Nowt!'

Ings frowned. 'It's going around. Let's go inside and take the weight off? It'll give you a chance to come round? Get warmed up?'

'No, lad, leave me be. I'll be alright. I'm better off outside in the fresh air. You've still not told me what's going on.'

Ings wondered what Wardell would do in his shoes. Would he play by the rules and keep his counsel? Or would he offer a snippet of information, hoping to elicit something further? Ings decided Wardell would dangle a big juicy worm, the gamekeeper would find irresistible.

'We've been lifting floorboards in the headmaster's study,' Ings said, studying Stan's reaction. Ings thought he saw a fleeting nuance of understanding behind bloodshot eyes.

'Oh, aye?'

'Yes. We've had a tip-off. Someone, an ex-pupil, told us we'd find something interesting hidden in the floor void, next to the window.'

Stan's eyes widened. He hesitated before speaking. 'And have you found owt, yet?'

'We have, yes.'

'I see. If you don't mind me asking, only, is it what you were expecting to find?'

'On first inspection, yes, it is. We've work to do. And, of course, a thorough forensic examination to undertake.'

Stan sniffled. 'That'll be standard procedure these days, I expect?'

'That's right.'

'So have you opened it, yet?' Stan said, covering his mouth, realising the implication behind his words.

'Opened what? I never said we found anything that needed opening.'

Stan frowned, eyelids batted. 'Clever bugger thee, aren't tha?'

'I like to think I have my moments.'

'I bet you do.'

'Mr Oldroyd. Stan. Why don't we go somewhere warm? Somewhere out of the chill? Have a hot drink? You look like you could do with a strong coffee. Then you can tell me everything you know about the Quality Street tin we found lodged between the floor joists in the headmaster's study.'

Stan nodded. 'Follow me, lad. We'll get a brew on at my place. I don't enjoy going in there.' A nod towards the school. 'It's long overdue that the truth came out. C'mon, Mr Clever Bugger copper, follow me.'

A chuckling Ings fell into step behind Stan.

23

TUESDAY 6TH JANUARY 2015, 12.45 P.M

Minster Mews Retirement Home was located in the leafy suburbs on the outskirts of York. Wardell and Watts drove into the southern outskirts from the A64 with Watts at the wheel of the unmarked Mondeo. The satnav showed their destination half-a-mile and two streets ahead, on the left. Dragging Watts on the indicator, Watts spun the steering wheel left and turned into a tree-lined residential street. Imposing brick 1930s villas sat either side of neat grass verges behind security gates, CCTV cameras warded off potential miscreants.

'What number are we looking for?' Wardell asked, scanning the house numbers. 'Monied up, or what? Their council tax bills don't bear thinking about.'

'Twenty-five, boss. The satnav's saying it's on your side, towards the bottom of the cul-de-sac.'

'OK.' Wardell nodded. 'We've just passed fifteen.'

They drove on.

Wardell counted out the odd numbers. Watts slowed the car and braked to a halt at a three-storey, double-fronted, 1930s, bay-windowed, red brick villa behind a gravel drive. Mature rhododendrons, skeletal oaks and spindly birches bordered the gravel. Several bins in an array of colours with the house number in a neat line under the trees. A sign at the entrance proclaimed 'Minster Mews Retirement Home Established 1985.' The house possessed a seen-better-days aura: paint flaked from the timber work, vegetation sprouted from the gutters and up through the gravel. Plasterboard offcuts heaped alongside the bins.

'Here it is, twenty-five,' Wardell said. 'Park next to yellow Deux Chevaux.'

'Ooh la la,' quipped a grinning Watts.

Watts swung the Mondeo left through a pair of tall brick pillars and brought the Mondeo to a stop alongside a canary-yellow Citroen 2CV with the nose of the car almost touching a stone mullioned bay window.

Killing the engine, dragging on the handbrake, his gaze met an elderly woman's sat in a high-back chair in the bay window. Watts, uncomfortable under her vacant gaze, looked away.

'Don't look now, boss, only... We're being watched.'

'I noticed,' Wardell said. 'Miss Faversham, she's only got eyes for you. Did you forget to switch your fanny magnet off?'

'Hilarious,' Watts said, stealing a glance. 'Christ, she is too. Women, they find me irresistible. I mean, who can blame them? The burdens I have to shoulder.'

'Being delusional is the only burden *you* have to shoulder.'

'Isn't envy one of the seven deadly sins, boss?'

'As I say, delusional,' Wardell said, reaching for the door. 'C'mon, let's get this over with.'

'How do you want to play this? With the priest, I mean?'

'We had better go easy on him. No point in steaming in, getting his back up. He'll only clam up. He's an old man. We don't want to bring on a coronary.'

'Yes, boss,' Watts growled. 'I mean, no, boss. If only half of McNiff's allegations are true, prison's too good for him.'

Wardell stalled his hand on the handle, turned to Watts. 'David, he's innocent until proven guilt. Let's try to keep an open mind. Alright?'

'Alright,' Watts replied. 'Still...'

'Still nothing... C'mon. Kid gloves, and that's an order.'

Wardell rolled out of the car, crossed to the front door, rang the bell, and lowered his mouth to the intercom.

'Can I help you?' An unseen plummy female voice asked.

'Good morning. I phoned earlier. I'm Detective Inspector Alan Wardell. This is my colleague, DS David Watts. We're meeting Mrs Vaughan at one.'

'One moment, please.'

Silence. Wardell looked to Watts, lips pursing into an annoyed pout. Two minutes passed. Wardell, becoming impatient, lowered his mouth to the intercom. As he was about to speak, the door lock clicked.

'About bloody time,' Wardell grumbled.

'Push on the door,' barked on unseen female.

The two detectives passed into a hallway-cum-reception area decorated with peacock print wallpaper above waist-high mahogany panelling. Fluorescent tubes buzzed. Keyboard keys rattled. The scent of pot-pourri heavy in the air. The receptionist sat behind the desk, typing with her head down. The rattle of keys ceased. Wardell and Watts strode over. The receptionist looked up, forced a smile.

Wardell showed his warrant card and the receptionist slipped off reading glasses and settled them on her chest. She studied Wardell's identification with weary indifference.

'DI Wardell. DS Watts. Here to see Mrs Vaughan.'

'You've told me that already. Please take a seat. I'll see if Margaret is available.'

Ten minutes later a door groaned open along the hallway. Wardell watched a short, dark-haired woman step into the corridor carrying a mobile phone. She glided towards them without looking up from the phone. She wore faded blue jeans, a white v-neck t-shirt and trainers. Wardell thought her more student than a professor. Watts thought her the male of the duo. Coming toward the seated detectives, she looked up and smiled the thinnest of smiles.

'Apologies about your wait, gentlemen. It's been one of those days. We've had a ruckus to sort. It's only just calmed down. We'll talk about it in my office.' She turned to the receptionist. 'Would you mind organising drinks, Sally? Tea and coffee.'

'Yes, Mrs Vaughan. Biscuits?'

'Gentlemen?' asked Vaughan, turning to Wardell and Watts.

They nodded. 'Thanks,' Wardell said, flatly. 'That would be nice.'

'OK, if you'd like to follow me.'

Entering the office, Vaughan passed behind the desk and settled herself into a leather recliner. Gestured with a rolled of the hand. 'Gentlemen, take a seat.'

'Thank you,' Wardell and Watts said in unison.

Once they were all seated, a brief smile played across Vaughan's lips. Shuffling forward, she perched on the edge of the desk and folded her arms under petite breasts. She studied the two detectives with an eager, curious expression.

'I'm very sorry, gentlemen, but you've had a wasted journey,' she said, without preamble.

Wardell glared. 'And why would that be, Mrs Vaughan?'

'I understand you'd like to interview Father O'Connell.'

'That's correct,' Wardell said. 'That's the reason we're here.'

'Thing is, Inspector, Father O'Connell isn't in the best of health. He's a Type 1 diabetic. He also suffers from acute angina. It's a common side effect of the diabetes. He experiences unexpected, often very severe mood swings. His hypo attacks present themselves in aggressive behaviour. I'm led to believe such behaviour is not uncommon in elderly diabetics. Today's hypo attack was severe.'

'Aye, I bet it is!' Watts blurted.

Wardell's flaring eyes instantly settled on Watts. Clearing his throat, he returned his attention to Vaughan. 'Severe, you say?' he said.

The door swung open. The receptionist stepped into the room carrying a tray with crockery and biscuits.

'There you go,' she said, placing the tray on a side table. 'Is there anything else I can get for you, Mrs Vaughan?'

'That will be all for now, Sally. You're an absolute gem.'

Sally turned, stepped to and dragged the door closed behind her.

Wardell inched forward, gave Vaughan the eye. 'Mrs Vaughan. When did Father O'Connell have his last hypo attack?'

'You mean before today?'

'Yes. Before today.'

Vaughan's forehead creased into deep folds. 'Now, let me think... If my memory serves me right, his last attack must've been around two months ago.' Quietening, momentarily, she doubted herself. 'Yes, that would be about right, two months ago. I remember it because the Bishop had just left. Father O'Connell became agitated. Demanded, we take him to a public house. Obviously, given his age and medical condition, it was out of the question. He wasn't best pleased. He swore. When he's riled, Father O'Connell can curse with the best of them. Then, when we thought he couldn't get any worse, he started lashing out. I had no option but to order two of the male care assistants to restrain him. We locked him in his room for his own safety. I hate it when it gets to that. Thankfully, it doesn't happen too often.'

'Yes, I can only imagine,' Wardell said, in as conciliatory a tone as he could muster. 'Today's hypo, when did it start?'

'When I told him you were coming to interview him. He was

much worse than before. We struggled to get him under control. This time, I had no option, but to sedate him with drugs. We gave him twenty milligrams of Diazepam. It's an awful drug. That said, I'll be the first to admit, it has its uses. As I say, it was for his own safety. At the moment, he's spark out in bed. Has been for the last hour. I'm not expecting him to come round for a couple of hours. I'm really sorry, gentlemen, that's why you've had a wasted journey.'

Wardell looked to the ceiling, mumbled, 'Bollocks.'

'Brilliant,' Watts said, heaving a sigh.

'Would you prefer tea or coffee, gentlemen?' Vaughan asked, taking to her feet to play mother. 'Don't stand on ceremony, help yourself to biscuits.'

24

WEDNESDAY 10TH SEPTEMBER 1975, 11.50 P.M

Colm crept up the staircase one tread at a time, leg muscles drawn as tight as bowstrings. Each tread counted, each potentially calamitous creak avoided. Arriving on the landing, he paused, drew breath, gathered his thoughts and exhaled through gritted teeth. Swinging the shotgun off of his shoulder, he tightened his grip on the barrel.

Downstairs, a clock chimed, a dry cough echoed, and a door slammed. Frozen by fear, Colm halted.

A long minute passed. Nothing stirred. The school slept.

Colm's eyes darted to the end of the corridor and settled upon the nameplate screwed to the door bearing Father Brian Murphy's name. Scanning left and right, satisfied, he set off along the corridor.

Arriving at Murphy's bedroom door, with the shotgun balanced across his chest, he opened the door an inch with his free left hand.

Peering through the gap he saw the dim glow of a nightlight. Neck craned right, his eyes adjusting to the semi-darkness, he saw Murphy asleep in bed. With a gentle push, he opened the door, stepped inside and closed the door behind him. With the latch clicking into the frame, he spun to face the room.

He stood in a bedroom, sparsely furnished with a single bed, bedside cabinet, wardrobe, a desk and chair. A crucifix hung on the wall above the headboard. The air in the room infused with the subtle aromas of incense and disinfectant. The only sound, Murphy's breathing, exaggerated in the room's stillness.

Colm crept forward and halted at the side of the bed. Leaning in, his breath ran over Murphy's cheek, and he whispered: 'Murphy... Murphy... There's someone come to see you...'

The sleeping priest's tongue slapped against his teeth and a throaty growl escaped his lips. He rolled over to face the window.

Colm drew a long breath in through his nose.

Stirring, not settling, Murphy rolled over onto his side toward Colm. Taking a step back, Colm dissolved into the shadows beside the door.

Murphy's eyelids stuttered open, and he reached out to the bedside cabinet. Fumbling, his fingers settled on the wire frame of his glasses and he put them on. Rheumy eyes discerned the dark outline in the gloom.

'Is someone there? Show yourself. I know someone's there. Don't think I don't.'

Colm stepped into the light. 'It's me, Colm.'

'Colm?' the priest rasped, coming to, yawning, rubbing balled fists against his eyes. 'Colm?'

'Yes. Colm. Colm Walsh. The father of the baby you murdered.'

'I see, that Colm...'

* * *

Father Flynn O'Connell sat in bed propped against pillows reading a Dick Francis paperback. In the stillness, he heard the *dull boom of a shotgun discharging. Placing the paperback on the bedside cabinet, he heaved a weary sigh, ran a hand across his face and swung his legs out of bed. Another dull boom echoed through the night. O'Connell shuffled on slippers and set off for the door.*

'Oh, dear Lord!' O'Connell gasped, a hand rising to his mouth, a plug of bile capturing in his throat, swallowing hard.

Father Brian Murphy lay slumped against the headboard, half of his head missing. A mangled mess of shattered bone, minced brains and severed bubbling tubes strewn across the pillows. Thin strips of bloodied brains hung from the crucifix above the bed, like jellied eels in an East End pie shop window. Pink and yellow intestines covered the bedspread in broken fatty coils. Methane and cordite thick in the air.

O'Connell stalled in the door opening and cast a hand onto the jamb. Behind him, Sister Mary O'Toole and novice Evelyn Shaw craned past O'Connell to get a better view. Colm sat slumped against the wall beside the bedside cabinet, a smoking shotgun balanced across his lap.

'Did you hear the bangs, Father?' Sister O'Toole quizzed.

O'Connell spun around, glared, ushered them away and dragged the door closed behind him.

'Get back. Don't look. Look and be forever haunted.'

'What's happened, Father?' Evelyn asked, innocently.

'There's been an incident.'

'An incident?'

'Yes, an incident. Father Murphy. He's dead.'

'Dead?'

'Yes, dead. What part of dead don't you understand, girl?'

'Sorry, Father.'

'Colm Walsh is slumped against the wall with a shotgun

balanced across his lap. *I'm sure you can work out the rest. Now wait here. Don't come in. Do you understand?'*

'Yes, Father,' the nuns said.

'Good. God willing, I'll be out in a minute. If I'm not, and you hear a shot, then make haste and call the police.'

O'Connell pushed open the bedroom door, peered inside, turned and nodded to the nuns. Disappearing inside, he closed the door behind him.

Raised voices coming from inside the bedroom displaced the silence.

Several minutes passed.

The bedroom door creaked open. Colm – under an unseen hand – skittled across the corridor, bounced off the wall opposite and fell onto the unyielding timber floor.

O'Connell appeared in the doorway with a broken shotgun under his left armpit. Stepping across the corridor, he hefted Colm up off the floor and threw him at Sister O'Toole.

'Sister, get this wee gobshite out of my sight. Take him to the Chapel and lock him in the sacristy. Watch over him like a hawk. I'll be down as soon as I can. I need time to think.' Spinning on a heel, he glowered at Evelyn. 'And you, girl, go back to bed! This is all YOUR doing. Whore that ya are! Away with you! Get out of my sight, or you'll feel the back of my hand! Go! Go!' O'Connell bellowed.

'Yes, Father,' Sister O'Toole said, collecting Colm's forearm, steering him past Evelyn.

Coming alongside Evelyn, Colm dragged himself free of O'Toole's grip. 'It's done. I killed him. You ought to have seen him. Fucking coward begged for mercy as he held his guts in his hands. I finished him off. I made him suffer. I did it for you, me, but most of all, I did it for Tommy.'

Sister O'Toole boxed Colm's ears, twisted his right arm up behind his back and pushed him along the corridor. 'You're going to rot in hell, Colm Walsh. As God is your judge, you are. Now move!'

Colm, struggling free of O'Toole's grip, spun to face her, icy hatred burned in his eyes. 'Take your fucking hands off me! You're no better than them. You did nothing. By standing by you condoned their abuse. You stood and watched them murder our son. Heathen bitch, I hope you rot in hell!'

O'Toole punched Colm in the stomach, doubling him up and put him in an armlock. 'Shut your rattle and move!'

25

TUESDAY 6TH JANUARY 2015, 1.00 P.M

They sat opposite one another at the kitchen table in Stan's cottage.

'Let's get one thing straight from the off, mister clever bugger policeman,' Stan said. 'I had nothing to do with the bairn. Do you hear? Nothing.'

Stan slurped coffee, set the mug down on a placemat.

'I never said you did,' Charlie replied, holding the hot mug, enjoying the warmth.

'That's something, I suppose. It's best you and I are on the same page. Mine's a quiet life. A life I enjoy living. Just so long as I've got my dogs, my cottage, and my birds, I'm fine. And, before you say owt, when I say birds, I'm referring to the feathered variety, not them with tits and run-away gobs. This place isn't much, but it's mine. There's not many gamekeepers can say that. Me, I'm different. I'm *savvy*. I pride myself on being savvier than most. Got myself a nice little pension sorted, I have. Not that I need it, mind, since I'm not planning on retiring. I love this job too much. It's nice to know that I can if I want, though. Aye, it's not a bad position to be in, at my time of life.'

'Enough respect, Stan.'

'We're agreed on something, then.'

Charlie grinned, nodded. 'We are.'

They drank coffee without speaking. The wall clock chimed the hour.

'What do you know about the Quality Street tin, Stan?'

'Know? What I know is this... Inside, you'll find the body of an unborn – a boy. The poor little mite died because he was conceived outside of wedlock. Is that what your source told thee?'

Charlie nodded. 'Yes. He said we'd find a male foetus. He told us the mother was a nun called Evelyn. That, the father was the gardener's eldest son.'

Stan shook his head, smirked. 'Gardener's eldest son, my arse!' he boomed. 'He wasn't the father, not in a million years, he wasn't. He was a bloody shirt-lifter. Tried it on with me once. I gave him a clip around the ear, a kick up the arse, and sent him packing. He never tried it on again, he didn't. Not with me, Anyway. Rumour has it he couldn't sit down for a week. No, the bairn's father was a pupil. A cracking young lad called Colm. Full name, Colm Walsh. I took him under my wing, I did. Taught him field craft, how to hunt, shoot and fish. He was heartbroken when they killed his bairn...'

Stan blinked, sighed. 'The headmaster, Father Flynn O'Connell, spun me a yarn. He said Evelyn had miscarried. Of course, it was a lie. They killed the poor little mite. One of the novice nuns told me all about it in confidence. It broke Colm's heart when the heartless bastards told him it was a boy. Poor lad was only fifteen. They sent the mother – the novice – back to Ireland in disgrace. That didn't help any. First losing the baby, then losing her. They were madly in love. He was never the same after. He became morose, got all maudlin. Nothing I said, or did, helped. It was bloody tragic. They're heartless bastards, them priests and nuns.' A solitary tear meandered down Stan's right cheek. Scrunching his shirt sleeve into a palm, sniffling, he wiped it away. 'Look at me, a man of my age, crying like a bloody bairn. Soft bugger, I am.'

Charlie closed his notebook and slipped it into a jacket pocket. 'You're not soft, Stan. You're human. It shows you cared. It's something to be proud of.'

'Aye, I suppose you're right. I try to look out for them lads, you know. I can't imagine how it must feel dumped in that bloody place at eleven years of age. They're not long off the tit at that age.'

Charlie nodded. 'Stan, I'm sorry, but I've got to get back to the office. I'll leave you be for now. With your permission, I'd like to come back and talk to you again. Would that be alright?'

'Aye, lad, it would. Owt that'll help set things right, then I'm more than happy to help.'

Charlie got up from the table. 'I'll see you anon then. Take care of yourself, Stan.' Charlie looked to the open gun cabinet. 'You be careful around that little lot. Guns can do a lot of damage.'

Stan chuckled, grinned. 'I know how to handle a bloody gun, lad. I should do. I've been around them all my life. I've told them that need to know: when I pop my clogs, I want my guns buried with me. If I find out they've not respected my wishes, I'll come back and haunt them. Then they'll wish they'd buried old Stan with his guns.'

'Yes, I expect they will. Goodbye, Stan. Take care of yourself.'

'You too, lad, you too.'

26

TUESDAY 6TH JANUARY 2015, 2.00 P.M

Bina Kaur parked on the edge of the city centre in a council-run car park recommended by Charlie Ings. Charlie had warned her to take plenty of loose change, yet still she found herself short of the eight pounds needed for three hours parking. *Who carries eight quid in change? Profiteering sods!* Bina cursed. A svelte, metallic-black Mercedes coupe on German plates, pulled into a space across the car park. Sheltering under an umbrella, Bina jogged over. To Bina's relief, the woman spoke perfect English and had plenty of change.

Exiting the car park on foot, Bina swung right into a cul-de-sac of townhouses terminating in an ivy-clad stone archway: The River Ouse visible through the archway. She passed through the archway, turned left onto the riverside path, and marched toward the city centre. The sludge-brown Ouse flowed past at a jog on her right. A sign indicated the city centre, half-a-mile away. Bina, head bowed against the drizzle, dodged puddles, mooring hooks and preoccupied Nikon-swinging Japanese tourists.

Arriving at Lendal Bridge, she grabbed the handrail and climbed the worn-to-glass cantilevered stone staircase to road level. Catching a breath, she ducked into a bus shelter to get out of the rain. Shared a smile with two elderly women sat on the rail along the glass back wall.

Taking out her phone, Bina tabbed to email. The ever efficient Marjorie had come up trumps. Marjorie's email listed the postal addresses of York's two homeless hostels. She highlighted the first of the two postcodes and copy pasted it into a satnav app. The small screen blinked, refreshed and displayed the walking route, just three hundred yards away.

Bina, committing the route to memory, plunged the phone deep into a pocket, said her goodbyes and stepped out into the rain.

* * *

Striding along the pavement, with the satnav in her pocket confirming, 'DESTINATION REACHED,' and a laminated sign in a ground-floor window announcing '*Jorvik Homeless Hostel*', Bina halted and gazed up at the facade of a four-storey, Georgian townhouse. Allowing herself a relieved smile, she took the short flight of steps two treads at a time. At the top, she paused on the threshold and shook off the rain from her shoulders and hair. Having regained her composure, she pressed the intercom.

'Hullo?' rasped a treacle-thick Glaswegian accent. 'Can I help?'

'I hope so. I'm Detective Constable Bina Kaur. I work for North Yorkshire Police. I'd like to speak to the person in charge.'

Bina heard a throat being cleared. 'Speaking. At least during daylight hours, I'm in charge here.'

'Sorry. I didn't catch your name?'

'That would be because I didn't tell you it. Name's Ali MacLeish. I'm the Day Warden here. How can I help you?'

Kaur placed her mouth against grille. 'Mr MacLeish, can I come in? I'm trying to locate a homeless man. Someone, I need to speak to, as a matter of some urgency.'

'You are, are you?'

'Yes.'

'Ten minutes. That's all I can spare you. We're rushed off our feet. We've fifty meals to prepare and time's against us. Two volunteers phoned in sick. You can't rely on folk, nowadays. When the buzzer sounds, give the door a good yank. Damn thing's been sticking. Come inside and wait in the lobby. I'll be a minute.'

'Thank you,' Bina said. The buzzer sounded, the electromagnetic lock released, and Bina yanked on the door. 'Appreciated.'

As she stepped into a metre square lobby of blank magnolia a rush of claustrophobia strangled the breath in her throat. She spun around. The door clicked into the latch. Too late. A security door ahead. On her left, a glazed hatch in two panes, one sliding, one fixed.

She heard a key turn in a lock and the hatch glided open. A hollow-cheeked, unshaven male face appeared in the hatch, dark circles beneath his eyes. He reminded Bina of a member of The Who. The tall, thin one, with the hook nose. The man's thin lips twisted into an impatient scowl.

'Would this homeless man have a name?'

'Colm Walsh. He's an ex-soldier. Until two years ago he served at Catterick.'

'That right?'

'Yes.'

'Alright. I'm going to need ID.'

Bina nodded. 'Not a problem. Is Mr Walsh here?'

'As luck would have it... He is, yes. He's in the kitchen peeling spuds. Or at least he was when I left him thirty-seconds ago.'

'Great,' Bina exclaimed, placing a hand on the door handle.

'Not before I see your ID, you don't. No ID, no entry. House rules. No exceptions. Sorry.'

'Sorry,' Bina said, removing her warrant card from her purse. 'Will this suffice?'

MacLeish inspected the warrant card. 'That'll do nicely. Pull on the handle, when you hear the lock release.'

MacLeish greeted Bina will a smile and curt instruction for her to follow him. He stepped into the kitchen with Bina following behind. A man, she assumed was Colm, stood over a pine table, peeling potatoes. He wore faded Levi's, a white t-shirt, and an apron printed with a pink bra and black suspenders. His forehead gleamed with a sheen of perspiration. The air in the hot kitchen suffused with the delicious aromas of roasting chicken, herb stuffing and baking potatoes.

'This young lady would like a wee word, Colm,' MacLeish said, collecting a pack of cigarettes from the table. 'She's a police officer whose name's slipped my mind.'

Bina peered past MacLeish to Colm, smiled. 'Hello, Mr Walsh. I'm Detective Constable Bina Kaur of North Yorkshire Police Major Crime Unit. It's nice to meet you.'

Colm looked up, then returned his attention to the potatoes.

'I'll leave you two to it,' MacLeish said. 'I'll be around the back, if you need me.'

Colm studied Bina with indifference, dropped a skinless potato into a blue plastic drum, turned, collected a tea towel from the rail, wiped his hands and returned the tea towel to the rail. She thought him leaner than in the photograph — more drawn, yet still handsome.

'Copper, eh? To what do I owe the pleasure?' Colm quizzed, hands on hips.

'Can we sit down, Mr Walsh?' Bina asked, gesturing to the chairs. 'Sit down and talk.'

'Yes, I'm sorry,' Colm said, dragging out a chair from under the table. 'I was forgetting my manners. Please. Take a seat.'

Bina unbuttoned her coat, expelled a cooling breath, sat down. She flicked open the two top buttons of her blouse and wafted air across her face. 'Phew. Is it just me, or is it hot in here?'

'Yes, sorry, you're right. I'll open a window. It's the oven. Damn thing's on the blink, again. I reckon it needs a new thermostat. Every five minutes, I have to open the oven door or it stops working.' Colm lowered into the chair opposite Bina. 'Can I get you something to drink? I was about to make a brew. The kettle's not long since boiled. It's no trouble.'

Bina nodded. 'A coffee would be great, thanks. Black. No sugar.'

'Coming right up.'

'Mr Walsh,' Bina said to Colm's back.

Colm glanced over his shoulder. 'Please, call me, Colm.'

'Alright. *Colm.* I'm sorry, but I'm the bearer of bad news.'

Colm glanced back. 'I assumed this wasn't a social visit.' The ting of metal against china echoed off the walls. Colm stepped over and set down two steaming mugs of coffee. 'These days, that's all I seem to get, bad news. It follows me around like a foul smell. To be honest, I'm getting paranoid. Weird, I know, but nonetheless, true.'

'I'm sorry to hear that, Mr Walsh. Colm.'

Colm sat down, sipped coffee. Smirking, sitting back, he positioned the cup against his chest. 'That's alright, DC Kaur. After Iraq and Afghanistan, I've developed something of a thick skin.'

'I can only imagine,' Bina said, reaching for the mug, sniffing the pungent steam. 'I need to talk to you about three things, Colm.'

'Three, eh? Blimey, this must be serious.'

'It is. Do the names Billy Searle and James McNiff mean anything to you?'

'Of course they do, yes. We were at boarding school together. I count Billy and Jimmy as friends. No doubt you know that, already. They're not in trouble, are they? The last I heard, Billy was working on a pig farm out Masham way. Pardon the pun, a mutual acquaintance told me he was as happy as a pig in shit. As for Jimmy, I heard on the grapevine that he's working as a bingo caller in Whitby. Jimmy was always good with numbers,' quipped Colm, chuckling at his own joke.

Bina's sombre expression betrayed words as yet unsaid. Colm, sensing her anguish, straightened his face.

'Something serious has happened, hasn't it?'

Their eyes met. Bina steeled herself. Looked away. Looked back. 'I'm afraid so, yes,' she said. 'Billy Searle.'

'What about him?'

'There's no easy way of saying this, so I'm just going to say it. I'm sorry, Colm, only Billy, he committed suicide.'

Colm felt a molten blade pierce his heart. 'That's a joke, right?'

'I'm afraid not. I'm very sorry.'

Colm fell silent, directed his gaze at the ceiling, placed both hands behind his head and pushed back in the chair, balancing it on two legs. A minute passed. He levelled the chair and stared, hollow-eyed, at Bina. 'And Jimmy? Don't tell me he's topped himself, too?'

Bina felt uncomfortable under his gaze.

'No. We're certain James McNiff didn't kill himself.'

Colm's mouth fell agog. 'So what, then?' bellowed Colm. 'C'mon, spit it out. What the hell's happened to Jimmy?'

Bina sighed. 'Colm, James McNiff was found dead at home on Saturday afternoon. Uniformed officers attended his address and discovered a body. The evidence suggests foul play.'

'You're having me on!'

'I'm very sorry, Colm, I'm not, no. I appreciate this must

come as a massive shock. I'm sorry, but both Billy and Jimmy are dead. An investigation into James McNiff's murder has already begun. It's the reason I tracked you down. Why, I'm here today.'

Colm fell silent, stared the thousand-yard stare for what seemed an eternity. 'Is this some warped bastard's idea of a joke, you coming here talking bollocks?'

'I only wish it were,' Bina said, in as sympathetic a tone as she could muster.

Colm rose, turned, stepped over to the worktop, stared out through the window and watched MacLeish stub a cigarette out under a heel, outside.

After a silent minute, he spun to Bina. 'Let's get a few things straight. One, Billy would never kill himself; he doesn't have the balls. Two, how was Jimmy killed?'

Bina hesitated. Her expression betrayed her unease.

'Don't hold out on me, DC Kaur. I need to know everything,' implored Colm. '*How* was Jimmy murdered?'

'Any particular reason you need to know the detail?'

'I do, that's all. You might as well tell me, I'll find out, anyway. I've got contacts in the army and the police. Don't you worry your pretty little head, I *will* find out,' Colm sneered.

What the hell, thought Bina, he had every right to know. 'You didn't hear this from me, right?'

'Right.'

'Someone shot James McNiff twice in the forehead at close range, with a small calibre pistol. He wouldn't have suffered.'

'Shot! Christ. Anything else?' Colm enquired, sharp blue eyes searing into Bina's brown pools.

Bina gazed past his right shoulder. Colm sensed she was holding out on him.

'There is, isn't there? There's something else, I can sense it. Something important.'

Bina swallowed, frowned. Met his wide-eyed gaze. 'Yes, there is. Colm, this is in absolute confidence.'

'Alright, I get it. I won't say anything to anyone. Scouts honour.' He crossed his heart. 'Cross my heart. Hope to die.'

'His tongue.'

'What about it?'

'Removed. After, I might add, his heart had stopped beating.'

Colm drew a long breath, released it through flared nostrils. Flames of anger and despair danced behind his eyes. He saw the scene. Imagined Jimmy shot, then desecrated. Bina thought he might cry.

'Poor bastard. Jimmy didn't deserve to die like that. Not after all he's been through, he didn't.'

Bina asked Colm to sit down. He obliged.

'Mr McNiff came to us with a statement. He called it a statement of fact. It contained allegations of physical and sexual abuse inflicted by the priests and nuns at St Aubert's. Colm, is there any truth to these allegations? Please, before you say anything, I want you to consider your answer with care.'

Colm sat back. Sniffled. Folded his arms across his chest. His head sank to his chest. Lost in thought, he gazed at the table top.

'Colm?'

'Alright! Alright! I heard. Jesus Christ, are you always this pushy? You're like a dog with a bone. Christ's sake, chill out. I'm thinking. It's a lot to take in.'

Bina looked off. 'I'm sorry. I didn't mean to upset you.'

A silent minute passed.

'The answer to your question is, no. Jimmy had an overactive imagination. That's the real reason you're here, isn't it? You're here to quiz me about these spurious allegations? See whether I'm prepared to corroborate them?'

Bina elected honesty. 'In part, yes. That, and to inform you we *are* considering taking you into protective custody. We've every reason to believe your life may be in great danger.'

Colm stood, picked up a knife, wiped it clean and collected a potato. He averted his eyes from Bina's.

'Protective custody, thanks, but no thanks. I take it you've said everything you came here to say? These spuds won't peel themselves.'

'I appreciate that, but we need to discuss this further,' Bina said. 'Please... Colm... Don't freeze me out.'

Colm interrupted Bina with a raised palm and a death stare. 'Why? You've said more than enough. Ugh, protective custody... Don't make me laugh. I'll look after myself, thanks. Isn't it time you were leaving? I don't want to be rude, only I've important work to do.'

Bina rose, slipped on and buttoned up her overcoat. Collecting her handbag, she said: 'Mr Walsh, we'll be in touch again soon. In the meantime, I'd ask that you take sensible precautions.'

'Don't worry about me, DC Kaur. I can look after myself, as quite a few Iraqi insurgents, and Afghan Taliban, would attest, if only they were alive to do so.'

27

TUESDAY 6TH JANUARY 2015, 4.00 P.M

Thump. Thump.

Father Flynn O'Connell banged the end of the rubber-tipped walking stick against the timber floor.

Thump. Thump. Thump.

The thuds continuing increased in volume and frequency.

Care assistant Mick Wallace snarled, dragged his feet down from the coffee table, bolted up and dropped the magazine onto the table. Stepping right, he stood and leered down at colleague Ashley: a teenage waif with spots and attitude. Ashley flicked him a glance, smirked and yawned.

'Listen to him. Old bastard's at it again. He's doing my bloody head in. You go, Ash,' Mick said. 'It's your turn.'

Ashley stared straight ahead and casually turned a page of HELLO magazine.

'Ash. You listening?'

Ashley turned another page, gave Mick a lazy two-fingered salute. 'Nope. I've seen to him twice already, today,' she said. 'What did your last slave die of?'

'I strangled her. On account of her insolence.'

'Hilarious.'

'Bollocks. I'll go. If you hear a ruckus, come running. OK?' Ashley turned a page. 'Ash!'

'OK! OK! Keep your bloody hair on. If he kicks off, page me.'

Tutting, Mick headed for the door.

Striding along the corridor, he whistled the Blackadder theme and halted at O'Connell's bedroom.

The thumps started up, again.

Mick placed his mouth to the door. 'Give it a rest, Father. I'm here already,' he shouted. 'I've heard. I'm not bloody deaf, you know.'

Opening the door, switching on the light, Mick saw a dishevelled O'Connell, back slumped against a high stack of pillows, his eyes staring blankly at the wall opposite. A walking stick dangling from the gnarled fingers of his left hand.

O'Connell's neck gyrated to Mick. The old man snarled. Wafer thin lips curled back and revealed rows of broken and buckled yellowing teeth.

'You're a bunch of bastards and make no mistake. Drugging and locking up an old man like a common criminal, does it give you a hard on does it? Rotten bastards you'se are,' spat O'Connell. 'When the Bishop finds out you drugged me, he'll have you eating humble pie. That, my friend, is a promise.'

Mick stepped over to the bed, lifted the walking stick away and settled it in a corner.

'Settle down, Father. That aggressive streak of yours will get you nowhere. We gave you something to calm you down. It was for your own good. You'd got yourself into a right old lather about the Old Bill visiting. Don't you remember?'

'I remember, eejit. I'm not senile just yet. Fetch me some water. I've a terrible taste in my mouth. I've a mind to sue for neglect.' The priest snapped like a cornered pit bull.

'Yeah, yeah, whatever,' Mick said, shrugging. 'Relax, Father. Life's too short.'

'Feck off!'

'Have it your own way. I'll be back in a minute.'

Mick returned carrying a plastic cup brimmed with water. He feigned to pass it to O'Connell, stalled his hand an inch from his fingers.

'Promise, you'll behave.'

'Go fuck yourself,' O'Connell grumbled, turning away. 'Moron.'

'No promise. No water. It's that simple.'

An indignant O'Connell directed his gaze out of the window for an interminable minute.

His neck spun, Exorcist-like, towards Mick. 'You damned heathen!'

Mick set the plastic cup on the floor. 'Why does the Old Bill want to talk to you, Father? I've been giving it a lot of thought. And I keep coming up with the same answer.'

'Oh, you do, do you? And what answer would that be?'

'You were a kiddy fiddler, weren't you, father? A kiddy fiddler like the ones in the papers. I'd put money on it. I read your file, Father. And, surprise, surprise, you used to be a headmaster at a boys' boarding school. Plenty of opportunities there to indulge yourself, I reckon. You must have thought you'd died and gone to heaven. I reckon you're a dirty fucking paedo bastard, aren't you, Father? The type that gets off on boys. You sick fuck. Yeah, that's you right, you're a sick, fucked in the head, kiddy fiddler. I'm right, aren't I, *Father?*'

O'Connell closed his eyes. His chin sank to his chest. His breathing became wet, tortured and raspy, then stopped. Several silent seconds passed. His eyes sprung open and he leered at Mick. 'You're right. You're a very astute man. A clever man. You'd have won your wager, *Mick*. Are you a betting man?'

'No, I'm not,' Mick mumbled.

'Well, you ought to be. You'd be quids in. Have you ever thought about it yourself, Mick? Wanted to get your hands on all that supple virgin skin. Ached to touch and own it. To do whatever you wanted to do with it? Whenever you wanted to? I recognise something in you, Mick. I see myself in you. You're just like me. They say it takes one to know one. And do you know something, they're right. You're right, I'm one. At least, I *was*. I've confessed my sins to better men than you. I've made my peace with my maker, a long time ago. And do you know something, *Mick?*'

Mick gulped. 'What?'

'They absolved me of everything. All of it. They absolved me of every mortal sin I've ever committed. Everything! I'm at peace now. My conscience is clear. They're all powerful. Power defines everything. Do you know what power is, *Mick?*'

A stone-faced Mick shook his head. Horrified eyes fixated on the old man. His words died in his throat.

'No. I didn't think you would *know*. I mean, how could you? Now, I'd appreciate it if you'd stop playing the amateur psychiatrist and hand me some fucking water. I'm spitting feathers.'

Unconsciously, Mick had stepped away from the bed. He stood with his back pressed against the door. Reaching to the floor, he lifted the cup, stepped over to the bed and handed it to O'Connell.

The old priest devoured the water in a single gulp. 'Argh! Good lad. Now, run along and get me a telephone. I need to make a call. Don't you ever deny me anything, again. Deny me, and you'll not live long enough to regret it. I know some very powerful people.'

'I'll go get you a telephone,' Mick stuttered. 'I'll be two minutes.'

Mick returned clutching a landline telephone, plugged the cable into the wall and passed the handset to O'Connell.

O'Connell grinned, cold menace glowed in his eyes. 'Thank you. It's nice you and I understand one another. Be a good boy and fetch me a nice cuppa. And, while you're at it, I'd like some of that lovely fruitcake. The fruitcake that the old fella's daughter across the corridor, brings him. She came yesterday, didn't she? I've an all-seeing eye, Mick. I miss nothing.'

'She did, yeah. There's some in the fridge. I'll get you a piece.'

'Excellent. Don't forget to close the door behind you.'

Mick backed out of the room without looking back.

28

TUESDAY 6TH JANUARY 2015, 4.30 P.M

O'Connell dialled the number from memory.

'Is that you?'

'Ask yourself... Who else would it be?'

'Nobody, I suppose,' O'Connell said, pausing. 'They've been.'

'And who might *they* be?'

'The police. Two detectives from North Yorkshire Police Major Crime Unit.'

'I see.' Silence. 'I suppose it was inevitable. Did you do what I suggested?'

'Feign a hypo attack?'

'Yes.'

'Did it work?'

'Yes. It worked a treat. The manageress wouldn't let them anywhere near me. The heathens drugged me. They used Diazepam. I could have done without that. I'm bed bound. I can't feel my legs.'

'Never mind. So long as you bought some time. By the way, There's good news.'

'I'm very glad to hear it.'

'There's just the one left.'

'Who?'

'Walsh. According to our man, he's proving elusive. Don't worry, he'll get the job done soon enough.'

'Tell him to be careful. Walsh will put up a fight. He can be vicious when he wants to be. He threatened me once with a knife. I used to have to discipline him, often.'

'I didn't know that.'

'You don't know everything.'

'I know enough! Enough to know what happened at St Aubert's is a boil that needs lancing.'

'That you do. I'm sorry.'

'So you keep saying. Your remorse is unnecessary.'

'Should the police come again, what should I do?'

'Pull the same trick. They can't touch an old man with a medical condition without there being a doctor present.'

'I can't keep playing up. They'll get wise to it. Tire of it. I can't handle the drugs, again. I'm too long in the tooth.'

'You're going to have to. Keep me informed. I'll call you when it's done.'

'The last one?'

'Yes. Walsh. In the meantime, sit tight.'

'Should I go to the cottage?'

'Perhaps.'

'You don't sound too sure.'

'It's not what we planned, that's all. I don't like change. Change represents risk. Worry. Uncertainty.'

'I know, but...'

'But nothing! It's time you grew a pair.'

'I'm nervous, that's all. There's something else you need to know, something important.'

'And what might that be? Explain.'

'I took a call from Father Tom from the school. The police

visited the school and lifted floorboards in the headmaster's study. They found a foetus.'

'An unborn?'

'Yes. Hidden in an old chocolate tin.'

'Why didn't you mention this earlier? I could've got ahead of the curve.'

'I forgot. I'm sorry. It was Murphy's doing. It was a long time ago.'

'How could you forget? You're a fucking liability, you know that, don't you? Where's the tin, now?'

'The police took it away. It's preying on my mind. With your blessing, I'd like to commission him direct and have him recover the tin. Of course, I'll pay from my personal funds. I'd like your approval. That's why I mentioned it.'

Silence. Static crackled along the line.

'Are you still there?' O'Connell asked.

'Yes... I'm thinking. A man's allowed time to think, isn't he?'

'Yes. I'm sorry. I meant no offence.'

'Alright. Call him. Keep it short. Do it soon. About the cottage... I agree. Get ready. I'll send a car like I did before. Same as before. Midnight at the end of the lane.'

'Thank you. And, Bishop...'

'What now? I've got to go. I've pressing business to attend to.'

'Thank you. May God be with you.'

'And with you, my Son.'

The dial tone rang out. O'Connell dialled again.

'C'mon... C'mon... Pick up eejit.' Still nobody answered.

He set the phone down on the bedside cabinet, lay back and drew a long breath. As calm reclaimed him, he fell asleep.

Fifteen minutes later, he woke with a start and collected the ringing phone from the bedside cabinet and recognised the caller's number.

'Thanks for calling back.'

'You called. Why? Be brief.'

'I... I...'

The voice on the line was direct, aggressive, and originated within the sound of Bow Bells.

'You shouldn't have called. I report to the Bishop, not you. I'll contact him when it's done. You know the agreement. Photographs for the first one. And three tongues from the others. Proof of all four delivered to a specified location, at a specified time of the Bishop's choosing. Is it, is it not, the agreement?'

'It is.'

'Good. I'll call the Bishop when it's done. Three down, one to go. Adios, amigo.'

O'Connell mustered all his strength. 'Don't go! Hold the line! Listen! There's something else. Another task. The Bishop knows all about it. He gave his approval to add it to your commission.'

Silence. O'Connell pressed the phone tight against his ear, strained to hear against the hiss of a live connection. 'You there?'

'I'm still here.'

O'Connell exhaled with relief.

'Be brief, I'm driving. I'm not hands free. If the Old Bill sees me, it could get sticky.'

'The police visited the school.'

'And?'

'And they took something away. Something I want back. I need your help to get it back. I'll pay. Just state your price.'

'You'll pay alright. Before I give a price, what is this *something*? I won't commit until I know what it is, and where it's likely to be. Old Bill won't hand over evidence without a fight. I assume what you want back is *incriminating* evidence?'

'They'll construe it as evidence, yes. The police twist things.

They find guilt where none exists. I can't afford to take that chance. I don't think it'll be too difficult to get back.'

'I'll be the judge of that. What is it? Where is it likely to be?'

'It's a foetus in a tin. Likely as not, it'll be at the morgue in Scarborough. I'll do some digging, to confirm it's there.'

'You've said enough. I'll get it back. Text through everything you know. Wire transfer me thirty grand to the same account as before. If all goes well, I'll deliver it with the other four pieces of the jigsaw. Happy?'

O'Connell smiled to himself. 'I will be once I've got what I want in my hands. That's five things in total. Photographs. Three tongues. One foetus.'

'Yeah, five things. Well done. You're a mathematical genius,' the man snorted. 'It's a work in progress. I won't rush. Rushing causes problems. Tell the Bishop he can expect a call towards the end of the week. We'll finalise the arrangements then.'

'I will. And...'

'What now?'

'Thanks. You're doing God's work.'

Laughter. 'Yeah, right... I like that. I'm doing God's work. I'm a saint. I'll remember that.'

The line died.

Father Flynn O'Connell lay back against the pillows, grinned, and pressed the end call button.

29

TUESDAY 6TH JANUARY 2015, 9.00 P.M

DS Simon Jones of Humberside Police CID, inputted the incident into the HOLMES database, sat back and stabbed ENTER. The timer icon whirled and spun. Yawning, Jones rubbed gritty eyes. His day had already been long and eventful. Not every day did a decomposing body wash up on the banks of the River Humber. Especially a body with gunshot wounds and its tongue missing. Estimating HOLMES would take thirty minutes to identify similar crimes, he decided on tea.

Jones looked across the open plan office and saw his immediate superior, DI Tom Marston and, two desk positions away, DC Caz Lane with her back to him.

Jones stood. 'Anyone fancy a brew?'

Marston checked the time. 'Not for me, ta. I'd better get off. Cheers, anyway.'

'Caz? You bothered?' No response. 'Caz?'

Lane glanced back, smiled. 'Sorry, Simon, I was miles away.'

'That's alright. Would you like a brew? I'm making.'

Lane, a fresh-faced twenty-six-year-old and as bright as a button, swivelled to face Jones. 'Just a cup of hot water for me, please, Simon. I'm on green tea. My energy levels are going through the roof.'

'Cup of hot water coming right up. You sure, Tom? It's no trouble. One for the road?'

'Yeah, I'm sure.' Marston said, rising, pulling on a jacket. 'I best be off. Her indoors will wonder where I've got to. Goodnight, everyone. See you in the morning. Don't be too late. Work life balance, and all that guff.'

Five minutes later, Jones settled a steaming mug of hot water on the edge of Lane's desk. 'Be careful, it'll be boiling.'

'Thanks. Noted.'

Straightening, Jones glanced at Lane's screen. 'Dealing with anything interesting?'

Lane dropped a green tea teabag into the mug, shrugged. 'Nah, if only I were. I'm doing HOLMES input again. I hate it with a passion. A couple of petrol stations got turned over in west Hull late last night. Likely as not, it'll be smack heads. Not a hope in hell of finding a match. To be honest, I'm bored out of my skull. How about you? Dealing with anything that gets the pulse racing?'

Jones nodded, sipped coffee. 'For a change, yes. *Murder.*'

'Details. Give me all the gory details.'

'This morning a dog walker came upon a body on the north bank of the Humber. White male. Early to mid-fifties. Early stages of decomposition. Cause of death, gunshot. Shot twice in the forehead with a small calibre pistol. And, you'll like this bit... The tongue was removed. I'm hoping HOLMES will throw up a match on the MO. How the hell I'm going to fit a murder investigation into my workload, is anyone's guess. I assumed you'd have heard about it on the grapevine?'

'I heard a whisper, yes.'

'Poor bastard. What a way to go, eh?'

'Contract killing, I reckon.'

'You think so?'

'Shot from close range, wasn't he?'

'Yeah.'

'Bit of a giveaway, then. It screams professional. And taking the tongue will be a condition of contract. If not, then a trophy. You must admit, it's a possibility.'

'Mm, perhaps you're right. I'll bear it in mind. Do you mind if I share your thoughts with the boss?'

'Not at all. Is HOLMES still processing?' asked a wide-eyed Lane.

'Yes. By now, it ought to be almost finished.'

'With luck we'll, I mean *you'll*, have a serial killer on your hands. Have you considered that?'

Jones's blue eyes widened, his jaw set firm, brow creased. 'Shit! I hope not.'

Lane battered her eyelids, teased him with a coquettish smile. 'If you have...'

'Yes?'

'If you have... And you turn up a match on the MO...'

'Go on.'

'Will you swing it so I can work on it? I've never worked on a multiple homicide. It must be a real buzz. My all-time favourite film is The Silence of the Lambs. I can see it now... Agent Caz Lane in a race against time to catch a psychotic killer before he strikes again... Clarice Starling, eat your sodding heart out. If you'll pardon the pun.'

Jones bit his lip, shook his head, smiled a wry smile. 'Caz, someone shot the poor bastard and cut his tongue out. It's hardly Hannibal bloody Lecter, is it?'

'No, but it sure beats petrol station robberies. I've had my fill of those. Please, Simon, pretty, pretty please... Promise me you'll put in a good word.'

'Look, I'll do my best. No promises. You're irrepressible, you do know that, don't you?'

'Thanks. I'll take that as a compliment.'

'Yeah, whatever...'

Simon Jones returned to his desk, sat and reached for the keyboard. Pressed ENTER. The screen flickered, whirled and refreshed. A message appeared in the centre of the screen – ONE MATCH FOUND. A bubble of excitement burst inside his head. Placing the cursor on the message, he clicked.

Much to his surprise, HOLMES had found a near perfect match against the MO. A white middle-aged male murdered in his home near Whitby just three days prior. Shot. Tongue cut out. Jones's mind reeled. Whitby! Just ninety miles north!

Jones craned his neck around the low partition, cleared his throat to catch Lane's attention. 'Caz, take a gander at this. Your dream, it's just come true.'

Lane raced over to Jones' desk, leaned across him and studied the screen. Scan read the HOLMES report for James McNiff's murder.

'Bloody hell, the MO is damn near identical. Got to be the same perp. Well, I never... I mean, what are the odds? And Whitby, it isn't far away, is it?'

'Nope. Ninety odd miles as the crow flies.' Jones scanned the screen, hoping to find the SIO dealing with the Whitby murder. Moments later, having confirmed Wardell as the nominated SIO, he recognised David Watts's name. 'First thing tomorrow morning, I'm going to give my old mucker DS David Watts a call, and let him know we've turned up another body.'

30

WEDNESDAY 7TH JANUARY 2015, 11.00 A.M

His plan was simple: buy a baseball cap, blue overalls, a canvas tool holdall, stepladders, and gain access to the morgue on the pretence of being an alarm engineer come to rectify a fault. He knew the simplest of plans worked best when coupled with a cheery attitude, and the brassiest of brass necks. He carried a badge printed with a fictional name for such an eventuality. A hasty internet check gave him the name of one of the hospital's many facilities managers.

He pressed the doorbell, lowered his chin against the prying eye of the CCTV camera and stepped back from the door.

A pock-marked face appeared behind the vision panel. Seconds later, the door swung open and a beer-bellied man in a grey t-shirt, stained hospital greens and scuffed light blue Crocs stood in the opening. He held a bacon butty limp in his right hand. They exchanged nods of greeting.

'Yes?' the mortuary technician said.

'Morning,' said the faux alarm engineer with a broad smile. 'Keeping well?'

'Can't grumble,' the technician said. 'What can I do for you?'

'I'm here to repair a fire alarm sensor.'

'Alright. Any idea where? Nobody said anything.'

'Body store. Thing is... I'm desperate for a piss. Any chance I can use the gents, first?'

'Nobody mentioned anything to me,' he said, running a hand over his chin.

'Ugh, typical. Mate, Guy Phillips from Facilities Management called our office and reported a broken IR sensor in the body store. It's a common fault. IR sensors and the cold don't get on. Like a bloody idiot, I've left the job sheet in the van. Do you know, Guy?'

'Of course I do. I suppose you had better come in,' the mortuary technician said, stepping aside. 'Gents is the first on the right. Body store's at the end of the corridor. Do you need a hand? With the repair, I mean, not the piss.'

'I'll be fine, thanks. It's a quick fix. Replace the duff unit, a quick test, and hey presto, all being well, I'll be on my way.'

The mortuary technician gazed longingly at the bacon butty and sniffed the air. 'If you need me, I'll be in the staffroom. Eating in sterile areas is prohibited. Give me a shout before you leave. OK?'

'OK,' the engineer said, disappearing into the gents.

Two minutes later, he leaned in through the staffroom door. 'Thanks. I've had a quick peek. Sod's law, the sensor's positioned above the door. I'd appreciate it if you wouldn't come in.'

The mortuary technician grunted, nodded.

'Cool. I'll crack on. Time and tide and all that.'

Entering the body store, the frigid air and totality of the silence sent a shudder through him. He closed the door, rattled the stepladders open and placed them behind the door. Turning into the room, he waited until his eyes had adjusted to the gloom. He flicked the switch and an explosion of white light dispelled the gloom.

He faced a narrow rectangular room. Daylight leaked in through a strip window set high in the wall opposite the door. On the left, a bank of steel refrigerated drawer units ran to the ceiling. Screwed to each drawer a steel plaque etched with a unique alpha-numeric reference. A steel ladder hung from high-level rollers at the far end next to the window. A whiteboard on the far wall under the window indexed the contents of each drawer, names written in blue or pink marker. Whistling, rattling the steps, he stepped over to the whiteboard and ran a finger down the list, at DRAWER B3: UNKNOWN UNBORN MALE. ST. AUB'S. 6TH JAN 2015.

'You alright in there?' bellowed the mortuary technician from the corridor.

Returning to the door, he rattled the stepladders.

'Don't come in! I'm up the ladder. You'll send me arse over tit.'

A quarter minute of silence.

'Alright, I won't... You sure you don't need a hand? Honest, it's no trouble.'

'Yeah, I'm sure. Cheers, anyway. The repair shouldn't take any longer than five minutes.'

'Alright. Give me a shout when you're done. I'll be in the staffroom.'

'Will do.'

Heaving a sigh of relief, he slid over to drawer B3, took a firm grip of the handle and pulled. The door glided out. With the momentum catching him by surprise, he halted the drawer with a flat palm. A draught of chilled air swam over his face. Craning forward, he peered inside.

In the drawer bottom, inside a circular tin, lay an object, wrapped in white cotton and tied with parcel string, beside it an ancient, faded Quality Street tin lid. He estimated the object as ten inches long, and four inches wide: about right for a three-month-old foetus. Untying the string, he set it aside and unfolded the soft cotton. On the final fold, he stalled, drew a long breath and gradually revealed the contents.

A minuscule human skeleton lay curled on the cotton. So small it might fit in his cupped hands. Its bones so delicate, he imagined they might snap under his breath. So beautiful he felt he might cry. He breathed in. The dust of unrequited life caught in the back of his throat. He coughed under a clenched fist, glanced at the door and heard only silence.

He remade the parcel, secured the lid, lifted the tin from the drawer and lay it in the empty holdall together with the tin. Zipping the holdall, he tied the buckles, collected the stepladders and stepped into the corridor. He made his way along the corridor, paused at the staffroom door, poked his head inside.

'Finished?' asked the mortuary technician, looking up from a tatty-edged copy of GQ Magazine.

'Yep. Done and dusted. System's working fine, now.'

'Glad to hear it. I expect you need a signature?'

'If you wouldn't mind. I'm going to have to nip back to the van for the job sheet,' he said, heading for the door. 'Back in a tick.'

'No problem. I'll put the kettle on, shall I?'

'That, my friend, sounds like a plan.'

31

THURSDAY 8TH JANUARY 2015, 8.00 A.M

A new day dawned dry and sunny with a nip in the air. It took Amanda Phelan ten minutes to defrost her electric blue convertible BMW M3. Two hours later, she pulled into the mortuary car park, yanked on the handbrake and reached for the door.

Mortuary technician Dave recognised Phelan through the iced edges of the vision panel. 'Morning, Miss Phelan,' his gruff voice crackled through the intercom. 'What can I do for you?'

Jogging on the spot, Phelan leaned in, put her mouth against the intercom. 'Morning, Dave. I'm here to collect a body. Let me in. It's blooming freezing,' she said, breath billowing away.

Dave nodded. 'Sorry. Wasn't thinking.'

The door swung open and a smiling Dave stood aside.

'Brr, thanks,' Phelan said, stepping inside, with a cool box hanging from her right hand.

He leaned out, scanned left and right. 'Come alone?'

'Yes, I have. No need for a hearse this morning,' she said, showing him the cool box. 'I've come for the remains of an aborted foetus. No point involving funeral directors for one so small. This should do the job.'

He shrugged. 'Only unborn we've got is in drawer B3. Came in a couple of days ago from the boarding school in Robin Hood's Bay. Police found the poor little soul under the floor.'

Phelan blinked. 'You know about it?' she asked, surprised.

'Let's just say, I have my sources,' he said, with a wry smile, tapping the side of his nose. 'I'm not as green as I'm cabbage looking. Can I help you with that?'

Phelan returned a thin smile. 'If you wouldn't mind,' she nodded.

'Not at all.' He took the cool box from Phelan. 'Makes you wonder what happened to the poor little mite. Sickening what goes on in those places. The things you see on TV. Hear on the radio. They make your stomach turn. Them that mess with kids ought to be castrated. I dare say there will be a cover-up somewhere along the line.'

'I wouldn't know about that,' Phelan replied, keeping her counsel. 'Drawer B3, you say?'

'Aye, that's right. B3. Follow me.'

Reaching the end of the corridor, he halted, recovered a bunch of keys and unlocked the body store door. He marched over to row B, set the cool box down, and turned to Phelan.

'B3's the second one up. Shall I do the honours, Miss Phelan?'

Phelan nodded.

'Just don't pull too hard. I pride myself on keeping the bearings and runners greased. Smooth as a baby's bum, they are. You'll know if the drawer hits you. They've some weight behind them.'

'I'll be careful,' Phelan said, stepping past him.

Pulling on the handle, she stalled the drawer with a flattened palm. Raising up, she peered inside and saw nothing but shiny steel. Dave arrived beside her. Their confused faces reflected in the drawer bottom.

'Strange?' Phelan said, frowning, searching his face for an explanation. 'You said B3, didn't you?'

'I did. I don't understand...'

Ten minutes later, they had opened and checked each drawer, twice. Every cadaver has been accounted for. He leaned across the empty drawer, settled his disconsolate gaze on Phelan. 'I don't know what to say. I'm lost for words. I put the child in drawer B3. This drawer. I was real careful, scared I might damage it. It was so light and fragile. Where it's got to is anyone's guess?'

'You're sure you put him in B3?'

'Course I am,' he replied, indignation written in his face. 'What do you take me for?'

Best not answer that, mused Phelan.

She shrugged. 'Has anyone been in here alone, recently?'

A shake of the head. 'No. I'd know if they had. I'm not a complete numpty.'

'I never said you were. We all make mistakes.'

His right hand ran over his stubble-covered chin. The wrinkles on his forehead deepened Lost in thought, he fell silent. Several minutes passed. His eyes ballooned. He made to say something, then bit his lip. Thought some more. Phelan imagined rusty cogs turning.

'Now you come to mention it, there was someone... Yesterday morning, I was in the middle of eating my breakfast when I had an unscheduled visit from a fire alarm engineer. He came to replace a faulty sensor in here. It's not the first time FM didn't inform me someone was coming. I thought nothing of it. I left him to it. People hate being watched when they're working, don't they?'

'I suppose they do. Was alone the entire time?'

'That's right. He was working behind the door. He did the repair and buggered off without me signing his job sheet. I remember thinking it was odd. I mean, how was he going to get paid? You don't think...'

Phelan rolled her eyes to the ceiling, reached for her mobile. 'I've got to make a call. Signal's hopeless in here.'

As Phelan stepped outside, phone pressed against her ear, Wardell answered on the third ring.

32

THURSDAY 8TH JANUARY 2015, 9.10 A.M

Wardell checked the time: ten past nine, ten minutes after the planned meeting start time, and still no sign of DS Bina Kaur. Bina prided herself on her timekeeping. A movie of untoward possibilities and unthinkable scenarios played through Wardell's mind. The movie flickered and died.

'Five minutes, troops, then we'll make a start with or without Bina. Did she mention to anyone, she might be late?'

Blank expressions. Head shakes. Mumbled nos.

David Watts looked up from his phone. 'Expect she's caught in traffic, boss.'

'You're probably right, David,' Wardell replied. 'If anyone needs a top-up, get one. We'll start at quarter-past.'

A chorus of grunted approvals rippled around the room.

The door sprung open. A bedraggled Bina walked in. Marching over to a free chair, she set her handbag on the floor, shuffled out of her coat and settled it on a back of the chair.

'Morning, everyone,' Bina said, scanning the room for the boss. Wardell glanced over his shoulder from the tea trolley. Their eyes met. 'Sorry, I'm late, boss. Traffic's mad.'

'That's alright, Bina. We'll make a start in a minute. Would you like a drink?' Wardell asked. 'I'm making.'

Bina nodded. 'Coffee. Black. No sugar. Thanks.'

'Sweet enough already, Bina?' Ings said, smirking.

'Something like that, Charlie, something like that...'

Wardell set the drinks down and the room hushed. Expectant gazes settled on him as he spun to face the pin and whiteboards and the photographs of the victim, James McNiff. A diagram showed the relationships between the alleged victims and abusers.

Clearing his throat, Wardell drew a long breath. 'OK, now that we're all here, I'll make a start. I'm sure you're all aware of the purpose of this meeting. This is the second meeting into the murder of James Andrew McNiff. Uniform found the victim deceased at home in Sandsend four days ago. This inquiry will include an investigation of the allegations of historic child abuse. The abuse alleged to have occurred between 1977 and 1981 at St Aubert's Boarding School in Robin Hood's Bay. James McNiff came to us with a written statement setting out those allegations in considerable detail. It's fair to say, his statement is harrowing. In it, he identified other alleged victims. Our task is two-fold. First, we need to identify, apprehend, and secure the successful conviction of James McNiff's killer. Second, we need to either prove or disprove the allegations of abuse. You all know how important it is that we build a convincing, factual and compelling case. Our focus is to gather reliable, admissible evidence. Shortcuts, forget about them. There will be no fudging of responsibility. As always, we act with professionalism. The CPS and the courts demand it. As usual, Marjorie will handle administration. Is that understood?'

A murmur of assent ran around the room.

'Excellent... Ladies first.' Wardell turned to a slouching Kelly

Roberts, chewing on a biro. 'Kelly, tell everyone how you got on in sunny Hull?'

Roberts sat up, removed the biro. 'Waste of time, boss.'

Wardell nodded. 'Go on.'

'You asked me to locate McNiff's old school friend, Niall Daley. Once found, I was to establish if he'd be prepared to confirm or deny McNiff's allegations.'

'That's right, Kelly. And?'

'And, I hit a brick wall. Niall Daley was last seen at 8.30 a.m. on Thursday, the first of January. A neighbour witnessed him climbing into the back of a medium-sized white rental van. Just before he got into the van, she'd seen him talking to a smart dressed white male with a suntan. She thought it strange he got into the back.'

'For everyone's benefit, explain why,' Wardell said.

'Because the passenger seat was empty.'

'Did she notice the registration number?' Watts asked.

Roberts grinned. 'As luck would have it, she did. She wrote it down on her kitchen calendar. It's CY12 OWN. Marge did a VC. The van came up as a white Ford Transit Connect, registered to a van rental company based in Horsforth, Leeds. A white male booked the van out on the fifteenth of December for a month. He used the name Thomas Farley and paid in cash. The manager's description of him resembles the neighbour. I've checked the passport and driver's licence, he used.'

'Good. And?' Wardell said.

'And nothing came up on the PCN, Home Office computer and Interpol. Whoever rented the van, used an alias and fake documents.'

'So what you're saying is... No one has seen hide nor hare of Niall Daley for almost a week. The last time anyone saw him, he was in the company of a tanned white male using a false identity, for reasons unknown.'

'That's right, boss. Daley's last shift was on Wednesday: New Year's Eve. He finished work at ten, left at quarter past. There's been no contact from him since. The pub manager says it's out of character.'

'Did the witness seem credible?' Wardell asked.

'Yes, boss, very. Daley lives in a ground-floor flat at the end of a cul-de-sac. The witness lives upstairs. She watched me arrive from the balcony. Watched my every step, greeted me on arrival. Daley always lets her know if he's planning on being away from home. On this occasion, he didn't. She, too, said it was out of character for him. She seemed worried. Makes a lovely cuppa, she does, boss,' Roberts said, grinning. 'It's years since I've had a chocolate bourbon. Scrummy, it was, too.'

Wardell smirked. 'Thanks for the tip, Kelly. I'll remember that, the next time I'm on my jolly holidays in the council estates of west Hull.' Laughter rippled through the room. 'Good job, Kelly.'

Kelly nodded. 'No worries, boss.'

Wardell, collecting his mug, sank the remaining coffee in a single slurp.

'How did you get on at Catterick Garrison, Bina? Any luck tracking down Colm Walsh?'

Bina smiled with huge brown eyes. 'Good, yeah. I met with his former commanding officer, Colonel Tom Woolverton. Bit of a dish, actually. Anyway, he pointed me in the right direction.'

Wardell rolled his eyes. 'Which was, Bina?'

'A homeless hostel in the centre of York. Walsh is one of two live-in volunteers.'

'I see,' Wardell said. 'Did you tell him about the suspected murders of Searle and McNiff?'

'Yes, boss, I did. He got upset. At one point, I thought he was going to cry. They must've been close. I suppose adversity creates a special bond.'

'And the abuse allegations? Did you inform him McNiff had named him in his statement?'

'I did.'

'How did he take it?'

'He said that he knew nothing about any abuse, real or imagined. He shrugged off the suggestion. Made a point of saying McNiff had an overactive imagination.'

'He did?'

'Yes, boss. The thing is... I got the distinct impression he wasn't being honest with me.'

'What makes you say that?'

'Body language. The whole time he was talking to me, his arms were folded across his chest, and he wouldn't look me in the eye.'

'Interesting.' Wardell paused, frowning. 'How did he react when you mentioned taking him into protective custody?'

'He declined the offer. Said he could take care of himself. Now I come to think about it, he was abrupt, blunt, even.'

Wardell felt a frisson of annoyance stir within him. Perhaps, he wondered, he should have been more decisive earlier and insisted on protective custody for both Daley and Walsh? Time would only tell if he'd called it right. He pushed the thought aside.

'Is that everything, Bina?'

'Yes, boss. Other than... I told him we'd be in touch again, soon.'

'And we will. Excellent work, Bina. Charlie, how did you get on?'

Ings smirked. 'Job done. The End.'

'Spill the beans,' Wardell said, rolling his eyes, 'cocky so-and-so.'

'With the help of SOCOs and two council bods, I recovered the Quality Street tin from under the floorboards. SOCO opened

it. Inside, there was a human foetus – *a male human foetus.*
Forensics guesstimated it had reached around three months
gestation. Not scientific, I know, but it gives us something to go
on. The post mortem is at three o'clock tomorrow afternoon. By
then we'll know more. DNA testing is ongoing.'

'Excellent, Charlie. Did the priests and nuns co-operate?'

'Not at first, no, boss. Nothing I couldn't handle, though.
And, boss, there's something else...' Ings said, grinning, dangling a
worm he knew Wardell would devour.

'Spit it out, Charlie. Given the look on your face, anyone
would think you'd won the sodding lottery.'

'As good as. Whilst SOCO and the council bods were rein-
stating the floor, I nipped outside for a ciggy.'

'OK. With you so far. And?'

'And I got accosted by the school gamekeeper.'

'Gamekeeper? The school's got a gamekeeper?' Wardell
queried.

'Yes, boss. It owns near to a hundred acres, much of it woodland. The gamekeeper's an old boy called Stan Oldroyd. He's
worked there for forty years. Considers himself as the font of all
knowledge about all things St Aubert's.'

'He does, does he? Go on, you've got my attention now,
Charlie.'

Charlie nodded. 'When I bumped into him, he was half-cut
on whisky. I thought it was too good an opportunity to miss. I told
him a search was being carried out upstairs in the headmaster's
study. I mentioned we were lifting floorboards next to the
chimney breast. Intimated we'd found something, without going
into detail. Out of the blue, he asked me if we'd opened it up yet?
He came straight out with it. It was obvious he knew about the
tin. Then, after he offered to make me a hot drink at his cottage,
being the good copper I am, I jumped at the chance. It was Baltic,
anyway.'

'Noble of you,' Wardell said, 'go on.'

'We went to his place. He made a brew. We sat and talked at the kitchen table. I told him James McNiff led us to believe that the gardener's son had fathered the baby in the tin. He almost choked on his cuppa. He told me that was impossible. Said the gardener's son was gay. Said the father was none other than... Cue the drum roll...' Ings turned to Bina Kaur, tapped his index fingers on the edge of the table. 'Bina's new friend, Colm Walsh.'

'Walsh!' Wardell exclaimed. 'Do you reckon he was telling the truth?'

'Honest opinion, boss?'

'Yes,' Wardell said, 'what else?'

'Yes, boss, I believe he was. He told me how he took the eleven-year-old Colm under his wing and taught him field craft, how to hunt and shoot. Told me how devastated Colm was about the baby. How he was only fifteen when it all happened.'

Wardell swung his gaze to Kaur. 'Bina!'

She felt his gaze. 'Yes, boss?'

'Get yourself back to York, pronto. Take a swab kit and get a DNA sample from Walsh. Request the fast-track service from the lab. We need confirmation he fathered the foetus in the tin.' Wardell swung his gaze to Ings. 'Excellent work, Charlie. Excellent.' Wardell finished his coffee, marched over to and set the mug down on the tea trolley, returned and sat beside Bina. 'David, tell everyone how you got on tracking down Sister Mary O'Toole. I'll brief the team on our visit to Father Flynn O'Connell.'

Watts shrugged. 'I had no joy in tracking her down, boss. I spoke to an elderly uncle in Glasgow. The last he'd heard, she'd left the Church and emigrated to the US. He mentioned New York. He'd heard on the grapevine she was killed in a car crash fifteen years ago. I've emailed the NYPD requesting confirmation. I'm awaiting their response.' The instant David Watts stopped speaking, his phone rang. 'Alright, if I take this, boss? It could be important. Might be pertinent to the case.'

'Fine. Go ahead,' Wardell said, adding, 'We're almost through, anyway.'

Wardell turned to the team. 'Just so you all know, David and I drew a blank with Father O'Connell. Wily old fox played the too old, too sick, card. The manageress at the old folk's home wouldn't let us anywhere near him. We'll spring a surprise visit on him. So, next steps.'

David Watts bounded in. A wide-eyed, cat-that-got-the-cream expression betrayed his excitement. 'Boss, that call, it concerned the investigation.'

'Go on.'

'It was from an old mucker. Someone I lodged with him at Bramshill. DS Simon Jones of Humberside Police CID. A dog walker came across a body – a white male – on the north bank of the River Humber. They've identified him from dental records. Boss. Kelly.' Watts glanced first to Kelly, then Wardell. 'It's confirmed as Niall Daley. Same MO as McNiff. Twice shot in the forehead. Tongue removed.'

Wardell sighed. 'Damn and blast!' He turned to Kaur. 'What are you waiting for, Bina? Get your arse in gear and get yourself off to York. Charlie, go with her. David, arrange for Traffic and ARU support. Get a bloody shifty on you lot. I want blues and twos all the way to York. I want Walsh in protective custody before the Chief Super can say, *I'm going to have Wardell's balls on a skewer*. Don't take any nonsense from him. I want him under a twenty-four-hour guard, ASAP.'

'Yes, boss,' Kaur said, reaching for her coat.

'Let's hope we get to him before the killer does.'

33

THURSDAY 8TH JANUARY 2015, 6.15 P.M

Colm took a long satisfying drag on the cigarette and felt a pulse of super-heated air course to his lungs and a surge of nicotine grip his brain. Leaning out through the window, exhaling, smoke billowed into the sodium-smeared night. He thought the nicotine buzz an analogy for the transiency of life. Here one moment, gone the next, taken on the breeze.

Grinding the butt into a foil ashtray, he turned from the window and lowered into a threadbare armchair. Closing his eyes, he drew a long cleansing breath of invigorating fresh air and exhaled. He felt the day's stresses hatch, fledge and fly and the omnipresent terrors circling within his head, settle.

Lighting another cigarette, he sucked hard on the filter and his thoughts meandered to Billy, Jimmy and the priests and nuns of St Aubert's. He sat and pondered whether there was a connection between Billy's alleged suicide and Jimmy's murder. Half a minute later, he dispelled the notion as ludicrous. Finishing up the cigarette in a series of hard draws, he stood, set his weight on the sill and ground out the tab on the foil ashtray. Leaning out into the chilled night air, he gazed down at the bustling street below.

About to turn from the window, Colm's attention was drawn to a small white van which pulled into the kerb opposite. As the van's engine died, the lights extinguished. Colm turned, stepped away from the window, slumped onto the bed and closed his eyes.

34

FRIDAY 9TH JANUARY 2015, 1.05 A.M

Waking, Colm thought it a dream – a dream in which sirens screamed, blue lights flashed and tyres screeched. The screams and screeches fell silent, yet the pulsating dance of electric blue remained. A phantasm of images – of sound and light – rioted through his half conscious brain and behind his eyelids. He wondered if the lights and noises were real or imagined? Deciding he had imagined them, he dragged the pillow over his head and fell asleep.

Bang. Bang. Bang. Insistent. A gloved knuckle brayed on the front door downstairs. The braying increased to a crescendo and stole his torpor. Became louder, more urgent.

Damned homeless, thought Colm. *Zero respect for anyone.*

'Open up! Police!' barked a gruff, Yorkshire accented voice. 'Open the door. Do it, or it's going in.'

Colm cursed. Yawning, he dumped the duvet onto the floor and stumbled bleary-eyed over to the window. There, he dragged the curtains open and looked down.

In the street below, two marked police cars parked either side of an unmarked car. Pulsing strobes of blue light spun around the street. The dream made real. Uniformed police officers stood in a tight circle on the pavement outside the homeless hostel.

On the opposite side of the road, Colm noticed the white van from earlier. It pulled out, sped up, and disappeared around a bend.

From downstairs, he heard the door unlock, hinges creaking, white light spilling out. Pressing his left ear against the glass, hearing voices, Colm strained to decipher what was being said. As the conversation ended, he heard the dull thud of feet on the staircase, and a knock on his door.

'Colm, you awake?' Ali MacNeish whispered. 'Colm, it's me, Ali. Open up. I need to talk to you.'

Colm said through the closed door, 'What's up? Do you know what time it is?'

'Course I do. Old bill is here to see you. They'd like a word downstairs. You'd better talk to them. Otherwise, they'll wake everyone up.'

Colm turned on the bedside lamp, slipped on a crumpled t-shirt, dragged on pyjama bottoms and shuffled on a pair of well-worn sheepskin slippers.

'Colm!' The door rapped hard. 'You coming or what?'

'Christ's sake, Ali,' Colm said. 'Hold your horses...'

'Good. At least you're awake. It's that bonnie Asian lass who came before. This time, she's come mob-handed. Look out of the window.'

'Yeah, I know, I've seen,' Colm said, recovering a dressing gown from the armchair. 'What time is it?'

'A few minutes past one.'

'You're joking?'

'Nope.'

'Any idea what they want to discuss, Ali?'

'No. They'll only speak to you. Get yourself downstairs and

sort it, Colm. They're waiting in the lounge. I need my beauty sleep.'

Colm flicked sleep from his eyes, ran a hand over his face and slapped himself awake. 'I'll be down in a second.'

* * *

Colm entered the lounge. Two detectives, stood by the window, turned to face him.

'Colm. Sorry to disturb you in the middle of the night,' Bina said. 'Only we needed...'

Colm interrupted Bina with a raised palm. 'I should think you are sorry. What's so pressing, it couldn't wait till morning?'

'Your personal safety, Mr Walsh,' Ings said. 'That what's so bloody pressing.'

'Ugh! Don't make me laugh. I can look after myself, thank you very much. I take it you know I was a soldier for thirty years?'

Ings' eyes narrowed, and he steered his gaze to Bina.

'Yes, Colm,' Bina replied, 'we're well aware of your exemplary service record. Since we spoke last, there's been an important development. It concerns another school friend of yours. Sit down, Colm.' The timbre in Bina's voice suggested more bad news. 'We need to talk.'

Bina lowered into the leather sofa and shuffled forward onto the edge of the squab. Ings stayed standing.

'Please, Colm,' Bina implored, 'sit down.'

Colm hesitated, eyed the detectives with suspicion. 'OK,' he said, slumping into the armchair opposite Bina. 'This had better be good. You've damn near woken the entire neighbourhood.'

'We're well aware of that,' Ings said, glaring. 'Mr Walsh, we're concerned about your safety. We only use blues-and-twos during the hours of darkness when we deem it necessary.'

'My safety?' Colm said. 'You're irritating me now. What's happened? Spit it out.'

Bina studied Colm; took a moment to compose herself. 'Monday morning just gone, a member of the public was walking his dog on the north bank of the River Humber. His dog ran over to what the owner thought was seaweed. It turned out to be a body.'

Ings interjected. 'A dead body,' Ings added, with a flourish. 'A white Caucasian male of your age and build.'

Bina glowered at Ings.

'Quite,' Bina said. 'The thing is Mr Walsh... *Colm*. Humberside CID have made an identification.'

'Go on.'

'I'm afraid it was Niall Daley.'

'This can't be right.'

'I'm afraid it is,' Bina said. 'They recovered a wallet. In it was a driving licence and other identification. They've also got a match against dental records. We're absolute certain it's Niall Eamonn Daley. I'm sorry, Mr Walsh, it's him alright.'

Colm sprang up, loomed above Bina, jaw firm, lips pursed, an inch-deep furrow vertical between his steely glare. 'Let me get this straight... First, you lot reckon Billy topped himself. Then, not so soon after, Jimmy gets murdered. He's shot. Some deranged bastard hacks out his tongue. Now, if what you're telling me is true, Niall's dead too. Is that right?'

'Yes. That's right. I'm sorry, your friend Niall Daley is dead.'

Colm exhaled with a sigh, quietened, stepped across to the window, stood and stared. Several silent minutes passed. He turned around, faced the room. 'How did he die?'

'It's too early to say,' Bina said, gazing past Colm's left shoulder.

Colm's face betrayed disbelief. 'Ugh, that's absolute bollocks and you know it. What do you take me for? Jesus Christ, dignify me with a modicum of respect, please. You steam in here telling me you've found another one of my friends dead on a beach – the third in a week – and you expect me to believe it was natural causes? Niall was murdered, just like Jimmy. That's the reason you're here. You're worried the same will happen to me.'

Bina's expression answered his question.

'I knew it! The look on your face says a thousand words.'

'I'm sorry, I only wish I could give you more information, but I can't. It's above my pay grade...'

Colm interrupted Bina. 'That's lame, and you damn well know it. Sod this for a game of soldiers, I'm off upstairs. Get myself a stiff drink. I'll be down in a minute. Alright?'

'Fine,' Bina said. 'I must insist DS Ings accompanies you. As I say, for your own safety.'

'Whatever...'

Five minutes later, Colm returned to the lounge clutching a half-full tumbler of whisky in his right hand. Studying Bina through glazed eyes, he slumped into an armchair. The aroma of an expensive malt whisky hung in the air between them. Ings leaned on the door jamb, blocking the exit.

'So, you're wanting to take me into protective custody?' Colm asked.

'We are. Those are my orders. We'd like – with your agreement, of course – to book you into a hotel with a twenty-four-hour guard. I'm going to level with you, Colm,' Bina said.

'I'm all ears.'

'We're treating Niall Daley's death as suspicious.'

'Fuck,' Colm blasted, slugging on the whisky. 'I knew it.'

'Colm, your personal safety is all that matters now. You're going to have to trust me. We're progressing several lines of inquiry. Have you noticed anything unusual over the last few days? Anyone acting suspicious?'

'No. Nothing,' Colm replied, too quick for Bina's liking.

'You're sure about that?' Bina asked.

'Yes, I'm certain.'

An awkward pause settled in the space between them.

Colm spoke first. 'How long do you expect I'll need protective custody?'

'To be honest, I don't know. What I can say is, the evidence suggests we're dealing with a very motivated and professional killer. You of all people will appreciate how effective a professional killer can be.'

Colm settled back against the smooth leather, played the tumbler between his hands, lifted it under his nose, savoured the tones and sank the remaining whisky in a single draught. He placed the empty tumbler on the glass coffee table.

'Alright, I agree. I'll comply, but on one very important proviso.'

'Which is?'

'York. The hotel must be in York. My globetrotting days are over. I've done my bit for Queen and country, I'm a home bird now.'

Bina nodded. 'Alright, York it is.'

* * *

Colm bounded down the staircase two treads at a time and slid to a halt in the narrow hallway facing Bina, Charlie Ings, and two uniformed police constables. He wore desert-issue camouflage fatigues, a beret and desert boots. A bulging Bergen hung over his left shoulder. His fatigues pressed to perfection. Union Jack patches adorned each shoulder; WALSH emblazoned across his chest.

Colm recognised mocking disdain in the expressions of the police officers. The youngest PC – a gangly, ginger-haired, fresh-faced teenager – bit his lip, stifled a smirk, and looked away.

'Find something funny? Don't you lot recognise a war hero when you see one?' Colm said. 'Well? Don't you?'

'It's not a war situation, Mr Walsh,' Ings said, with a healthy dollop of sarcasm. 'Your attire. Don't you think it's overkill?'

'You could have fooled me! It's two, perhaps three nil to the enemy. Whoever it is, that's out there slotting my friends, they'd better be on his, or her, guard.'

Shit, thought Bina, *that's all I need – a trained and motivated vigilante declaring war on a professional, hit man. Armageddon on the streets of Yorkshire.* Wardell would do his nut. Bina moved forward, stalled her face just inches from his: stared him down.

'Please tell me you're not armed?'

Colm chuntered something indecipherable under his breath and returned Bina's glare. 'Of course I'm not armed. What do you take me for? An amateur?'

Bina dodged the question. 'I need you to promise me, Colm.'

'At the risk of repeating myself, no, I'm not bloody armed! Satisfied?'

'That's alright then,' Bina said, recovering car keys from her handbag. 'Now that's sorted, it's time we got going. You'll be travelling in the Mondeo with myself and DC Ings, in convoy.' Bina turned to the uniformed officers. 'You two, get going. Don't stop at lights.'

The PCs nodded and strode away.

'Where are you taking me?'

'The Castle Hotel. Know it?'

'The posh one on Kirkgate?'

'Yes. You'll be staying in the bridal suite. We've booked you in until Sunday. It's all they had available. You're a lucky man, Mr Walsh.'

'You think so?'

Bina studied Colm. He was getting on her nerves. 'OK, let's get going. Wait here. I'll signal when it's safe to leave.'

Bina paused on the threshold, glanced left and right along the street, and opened the car with the remote. She took the steps two treads at a time. Reaching the car, she sprung open the back door, turned and waved Colm and Ings forward.

Colm lifted the bulging Bergen onto his shoulder. Pausing, he felt the reassuring presence of the pistol hard and cold against the hollow of his back. He negotiated the steps, threw the Bergen in and dived into the car. In the dark cabin, he lay gazing at the headlining. Bina slammed the back door closed and climbed into the front passenger seat. As Ings swung into the driver's seat, the car rocked on its suspension. Colm heard the driver's door slam, the click of the steering lock disengaging and the roar of the engine. Seconds later, indicators clicked, and the handbrake groaned. As the car gained momentum, streetlights marched overhead.

'Stay down. We'll be there in five minutes,' Bina said.

Colm raised on an elbow, peered through the side glass and glimpsed the small white van. Driving past, he saw the outline of a man silhouetted in the driver's seat.

35

FRIDAY 9TH JANUARY 2015, 2.00 A.M

Bina turned on the light, stood aside to let Colm pass into the bridal suite.

The room featured an impressive four-poster bed, yew sideboards and cabinets. A pair of Peacock print rolled-arm sofas sat at right angles to a Louis XIV fireplace. Garish flower print swags and tails hung at the balcony patio doors.

Colm crossed to the bed, set his Bergen down on the floor. Straightening, he pressed his right hand deep into the silk throw and found himself surprised by the unexpected firmness of the mattress.

Bina watched him from the door, arms folded. 'What do you think?' she asked. 'I'm told it's the best they have.'

Colm lips curled, shoulders jigged. 'It'll do. Mattress is firm. I like a firm bed. Surprising given it'll have seen a lot of action, don't you think?'

Bina's face turned a darker shade of dusky brown. 'Mm,' she mumbled, with an embarrassed grin. 'I expect you're right. Settle in. Relax. Try to get some sleep. Make the best of it. Room service's available twenty-four hours a day. There's a police constable stationed outside in the corridor. He'll be there for the duration of your stay.' Bina drew breath. 'Is there anything you need to know? Anything I can get for you?'

He shook his head. 'Nope. I'll be fine. You make it sound like I've moved in permanent. Nice though it is, I hope my stay here is short,' Colm said.

'Yes. As I mentioned earlier, we're progressing several solid lines of inquiry. I'll call with a progress update every day. What suits you best, time wise?'

'Is there a gym?'

'Yes. In the basement. There's a pool, sauna and hot tub. Opens at seven. I checked.'

'Excellent. I'll plan on being up with the larks. Would ten a.m. be too early for you?'

'No. Ten's fine.' Bina checked the time. 'Given the time now, I'll give tomorrow a miss. Expect a call at ten, Saturday morning.'

'I'll look forward to it.'

Bina flashed him a smile. 'Good. You're sure there's nothing else I can get for you?'

'No. Nothing. Goodnight, DC Kaur.'

'Goodnight, Colm.'

Bina slipped into the corridor, set a hand on the handle, was just about to close the door.

'DC Kaur... Bina...,' Colm said. 'Thanks. I appreciate what a pain in the rectal area I can be, sometimes. I'm harmless enough once you get to know me.'

'It's all part of the service. Get some rest. If you need anything, give the PC a shout.'

Colm nodded. 'I will. Thanks.'

Bina pulled the door closed.

Colm collected the Bergen from the floor, settled it on the bed, flipped open the main compartment and reached inside.

Sleep was the last thing on his mind.

36

FRIDAY 9TH JANUARY 2015, 2.15 A.M

Colm placed his left ear against the door and heard Bina wish the young constable goodnight. Moments later, the startling ding of the arriving lift car and the rattle of the doors closing, echoed along the corridor.

Stepping away from the door, he padded to the bed and got undressed. He pulled on black Levis, a grey Ralph Lauren polo shirt and a tan leather box jacket. Zipping up, hands in pockets, he studied his reflection in the mirror on the back of the wardrobe door and felt the pistol firm in the arch of his back. Liking what he saw, he allowed himself a smile.

Turning, he slid the balcony door open and stepped outside into the chilly night. He leaned on the balustrade gazing across the amphitheatre of structures and buildings surrounding the hotel: left, a terrace of half-timbered medieval houses re-purposed as craft shops, bars and bistros; right of the terrace, the ornate yorkstone facade of the Old Gaol House; right of the Goal house, the imposing Romanesque columns along the frontage of The Castle Museum, ahead, Clifford's Tower: an impressive medieval stone keep atop a five storey high pyramid of grass, floodlit to reveal its full majesty.

Having jogged the vicinity most mornings, he visualised the hotel's facade. Leaning on the handrail, he looked down, eyes straining against the darkness. Satisfied, he stepped back.

The abseil through the matrix of balconies to the pavement took ten seconds. Landing unseen, he untied the rope and stepped into the shadows of a fire escape recess. Gathering breath, he felt a clawing dampness envelope him and the rank stench of urine and vomit assailed his nostrils. Throat tightening, eyes watering, he sank onto his haunches and gagged.

Composure regained, Colm leaned out and scanned the street. Seeing no one, hearing only silence, with no evidence that his unconventional exit had drawn attention, he raised up. About to step out, hearing footsteps, he sank back into the shadows, pressed his back against the unyielding brickwork. Every muscle taught as a drum. The pistol firm under his fingers.

From out of the gloom someone moved closer. Swayed. Halted. Cold sweat trickled down Colm's back. The gloom darkened. His grip on the pistol tightened. He held his ground.

Silhouetted by streetlight, the swaying figure belched an explosion of sickly alcohol breath in Colm's face, followed by a stream of incoherent profanities, the tip-tap of drunken dancing feet and the unmistakable metallic murmur of a zip being dragged down.

'Don't you fucking dare!' Colm hissed. Launching himself on to the pavement he shoved hard and ejected the silhouette into the street.

The silhouette revealed itself as a youth. He cast a steadying hand onto a lamppost, staggered and steered an unfocussed gaze back towards Colm.

The youth's vision cleared. He raised placatory hands. 'What the fuck you doing hiding in there, man? I just wanna pish... Tha's all...' he slurred. 'Sorry...'

'Be a good boy. Fuck off. Alright?'

The youth burped. 'Alright... Alright... Tha's... Cool... I don't want any trouble mister... Honest I don't...'

Spinning around, the youth tripped over a kerb and fell headlong onto the grassy embankment. Scrambling up, he spun to face Colm, glanced at his mud covered jeans and brushed himself down. 'Fuckin' hell... Look at state o' me... Mum's gonna do her nut when I get home... It's all darn to thee this is... Pillock...'

Colm, lunging forward, snarled like a wounded bear. The youth spun around and ran away as fast as his legs would carry him.

37

FRIDAY 9TH JANUARY 2015, 4.45 A.M

A deluge of anxiety flooded Bina's brain. She imagined Wardell's angst. Reaching into her handbag, she reclaimed her mobile and selected Wardell from contacts. The call rang out. She tried again. On the tenth ring, the line connected.

'Wardell,' he croaked.

'Sorry to disturb you, boss. It's Bina. I'm afraid there's been a development. Something you should know.'

Unfocussed thoughts coalesced in Wardell's head. 'One sec,' he said, swinging out of bed, rubbing sleep from his eyes, glancing at the bedside clock – 4.45 a.m. displayed in inch-high green digital numerals. 'What's up? This'd better be good. It's not yet five.'

'It's Walsh, boss,' a nervous pause. 'He's done a runner.'

A bowel-tightening silence settled on the line.

'Boss, you still there?'

Give me bloody strength, thought Wardell. *Heads will roll.*

'Yeah, I'm still here,' he growled, shuffling into slippers, dragging on a dressing gown. 'You sure?'

'Yes, boss, I am. We've checked and checked again. Looked everywhere. The hotel staff have conducted a thorough search, too. Everyone's accounted for with one notable exception... *Walsh.*'

'Christ's sakes, Bina! How and when did this happen?'

'I'm not sure. We're trying to piece together what happened. I took a call from PC Collins at half three this morning. He looked in on Walsh just before three. The room was empty. The door onto the balcony open. There's no evidence of forced entry. No signs of disturbance. His army uniform, boss...'

'What of it?' Wardell interjected.

'Stacked on the bed.'

Wardell pondered the facts. 'Seems our volatile ex-serviceman has gone AWOL, of his own volition.'

'Yes, boss,' Bina said, keen to placate him, 'he has.'

'Have you checked the hotel's CCTV, yet? They must have a half-decent system?'

'Not yet, boss. But I will.'

'Get onto it straight away. After you've done that, get yourself across to the council's CCTV control centre. See if you can track his movements through the city centre. He can't have gone far. In the meantime, call it in. Circulate his description. I want him found. I don't want him coming to, or doing any harm. Either of those two scenarios come to pass, the Chief Super will do his nut.'

'On it,' Bina said. 'And, boss...'

'What now?'

'I'm sorry. This shouldn't have happened. Walsh was my responsibility. I messed up.'

Wardell bit his tongue, hesitated before speaking. 'Don't worry, shit happens. There's no denying it's an almighty cock-up, but no one is infallible. You couldn't have watched over him twenty-four seven. Focus on the CCTV. The moment you find anything, call me. Alright?'

'Alright. Thanks, boss.'

'There's no need to thank me.'

Wardell flung off his dressing gown, stomped into the en-suite and spun the dial.

38

THURSDAY 11TH SEPTEMBER 1975, 12.30 A.M

Father O'Connell rapped on Stan's front door without reply. Stalling, cursing under his breath, he stepped out from under the protective embrace of the canopy and gazed across the facade. Autumnal drizzle licked his face, an icy chill ran down his spine.

About to knock again, a dim yellow light flickered on upstairs behind net curtains. Something moved, and the light dimmed. From beyond the front door, he heard the dull thud of feet descending a staircase. A moment later, the front door creaked opened arthritically and white light flooded out. O'Connell raised a hand over his brow against the glare. Stan in a raggedy towelling dressing gown, tartan pyjamas and blackened moccasin slippers, peered out from the threshold, craggy face bent into a sour scowl.

The wide-eyed, red-faced priest, woollen coat shimmering with raindrops, thrust a shotgun at Stan. 'Yours. I believe!'

'It is,' Stan said, accepting the gun. 'Ta.'

'Might I come in? It's enough to freeze a man's resolve.'

Stan continued to block the door, broke the gun, removed two spent cartridges, pocketed them and propped the gun in a corner, barrel pointing up.

'Did I hear gunshots? Seemed to me they were coming from the direction of the school,' Stan enquired, adding, 'Where's Colm?'

'So you knew he had the gun?'

'I did. And what of it? I trust him. The lad and I, we've got an understanding. He said he was planning on shooting vermin.'

'Did he now?'

'Yes, he did. What have you come here to say, Father?' Stan asked, leaning on the jamb.

O'Connell cleared his throat. 'It's a long story. Might we talk inside? I'm soaked. I'll catch pneumonia.'

Stan raised his chin, looked down at the priest along his broken, aquiline nose. 'Aye, I suppose you better come in,' he said, stepping aside. 'We'll sit in the kitchen. You look like you need a drink?'

'I do,' O'Connell said. 'You're a good man, Stan. God bless you.'

They sat facing one another across the kitchen table, sipping twelve-year-old malt from Waterford Crystal tumblers. Stan's fifteen-year-old collie, Barney, snored wet snores from the basket by the fire. The dying embers of the fire crackled and danced like fireflies on the updraught.

'Has something happened, Father? I hope you don't mind me saying... Only... Only you look like someone with something weighing heavily on their mind,' Stan said. 'Has Colm come to any harm? I look out for that lad. If he's come to any harm, as God is my judge, I'll...'

O'Connell interjected with a raised hand. 'Don't worry your head about Colm Walsh, he's safe enough.'

O'Connell, settling the tumbler on the time-worn pine, stared a dead stare at the dying embers of the fire reflected in the crystal tumbler.

A silent minute passed.

'I heard gunshots, Father. And, if I'm not mistaken, they came from the priest's quarters. I've an ear for these things,' Stan said.

'You're not wrong. That's where they came from. The boy lost his head. He's only gone and shot and killed Father Brian,' O'Connell said, matter-of-factly.

'Colm? Nay, that can't be right.'

O'Connell's withering gaze settled on Stan. 'Ask yourself, would I lie about something so serious? What reason would I have?'

'I suppose you wouldn't, no, you being a man of the cloth.'

'There you go. Father Brian Murphy's dead, alright, and it was Colm Walsh who killed him. He shot him twice. Once in the guts, and once in the face. Half his head blown clean away. Horrific, it was. Like a scene from a horror movie. God rest Father Brian's tortured soul.'

'What a bloody mess. Why would he do such a thing?' Stan asked.

'You mean you don't know? I thought you said you two were close?'

'The rumours... Are you referring to the rumours? Talk going round of kids getting touched.'

O'Connell's eyes rolled to the ceiling. After an interminable silent minute, he settled his gaze on Stan.

'Those rumours are nothing less than tittle-tattle, fabrications and lies. The boys imagine all sorts. I blame Sister Tomlinson's creative writing lessons. Truth be told, it's a lethal combination: raging hormones, young minds, vivid imaginations. I wouldn't believe everything you hear.'

'I see,' Stan said.

'Did Colm ever mention a baby?'

'A baby?'

'You mean to tell me, you don't know about the baby?'

'No.'

O'Connell fell silent, sipped whisky, settled the tumbler on the pine and held it firm under a hand. 'There was a baby. Five months ago, Colm had his evil way with one of the novice nuns. Before it had gone too far, by God's hand, she lost it. It was a boy. The Bishop decided it would be best for all concerned, if we sent her home to Eire. It was God's will.'

'I see... What a terrible mess. Poor lad must've been heartbroken. No reason to take a life, though.'

'You're right enough there. The novice was under Father Brian's care. When she got pregnant, she all but stopped eating. She lost the baby. That's when the incident occurred.'

'Incident?'

'Yes. I won't go into detail. All I'll say is, Father Brian had issues. Anger. Shame. Guilt. The thing is, Father Brian was schooled by monks. It always leaves its mark. One Sunday after morning mass, Father Brian and the novice, argued. She alleged he used excessive physical force. Of course, there were no witnesses to substantiate her claims. That same night, she lost the baby. No doubt it's the reason Colm killed him. He'll be holding Father Brian responsible for the miscarriage, I expect.'

'Christ, what a bloody mess... Sorry, Father, I didn't mean to blaspheme.'

'That's alright, Stan. You're in shock. We all are. You're right about one thing though, this is a terrible, terrible, mess.'

They gazed into the fire in silent reflection.

Stan spoke first. 'So, what now?'

O'Connell leaned in, made a low pyramid with his hands and placed them on the table. Their eyes met. 'Stan, I need your help and confidence. This mess needn't ruin a boy's life. If we work together – you, me, Colm – this whole thing, everything, need never leave this place.'

'What are you suggesting, Father?'

'I'm suggesting we give Father Brian a Christian burial. After-

wards, we need to sit down with Colm and discuss matters like adults. Somehow, define a future with a shared understanding.'

'Resolve things? Define a future? Shared understanding? You make it sound easy.'

'It can be. Bottom line is, you and I, we need to come to some kind of mutually beneficial accommodation.'

'In other words, you want to brush everything under the carpet?'

'If that's what it takes to keep Colm out of prison and protect St Aubert's good name, then yes, that's what we do.'

'I don't know,' Stan said, stalling. 'A crime's a crime. A man has lost his life.'

'Stan, you're an intelligent man. Think! It's imperative we keep this out of the public domain. If we don't, bad things will happen.'

'I suppose I can see where you're coming from.'

'If the newspapers get hold of this, Stan, they'd force the Bishop's hand. Eventually, he'd have no option to bow to the pressure and close the school. Everyone, and I mean everyone, you and I included, would lose their livelihoods. Nobody wants that to happen, do they, now?'

'No, I don't suppose they do...'

'A priest's died, Stan. We'll deal with it. The Church manages its own affairs. We have a code. A way of working.'

'Oh aye?'

'Believe me, it's true. Will you help me, Stan? Will you help Colm? He respects you. He needs you now more than ever.'

Stan sunk the remaining whisky, looked away, looked back. 'Alright, I'll help. As long as you – the Church – accept one, non-negotiable condition.'

'Which is?'

'This place...'

'What of it?'

'It's my home. The place where I want to see my days out. Father, I've lived in this cottage for twenty years, yet I don't own a single brick of it. Have you any idea how that makes me feel?'

'No.'

'It makes me feel small. Inadequate.'

'I expect it does.' O'Connell fell silent. Half a minute passed. He smiled wryly. 'So, let me get this straight... What you're saying is... As a condition for bringing Colm around to my way of thinking, you want this cottage putting in your name?' O'Connell said.

'I do, yes.'

O'Connell's face creased with thought. 'And you'll help me dispose of Father Brian's body tonight? You'll help clean up the mess in his bedroom? You'll talk Colm round? You make a solemn promise never to utter a word of this to another living soul?'

Stan nodded. 'I will. I want this cottage, Father.'

O'Connell offered his hand. 'Deal!'

Stan grinned.

The two men shook hands.

'Excellent. Just one more snifter of this fine malt to seal the deal and we'll make a start. We wouldn't want to keep Father Brian waiting, now would we?' Father Flynn O'Connell said, dark eyes sparkling. 'Not that he'd notice, of course.'

Stan nodded. 'No, I don't suppose he would.'

39

FRIDAY 9TH JANUARY 2015, 5.00 A.M

Bina hurried through the city centre to the council building housing the CCTV Control Centre. The stone-built Georgian building sat behind cast-iron railings on the inner ring road.

Arriving at the double entrance doors, she pressed the intercom, stepped back and studied her reflection in the fish-eyed CCTV camera bolted to the wall above the door. A distorted Martian balloon head perched on a serpent's body looked back. She felt watched, studied. She pressed the intercom again and stepped back.

The intercom burst to life. 'Hello. Can I help you?'

'I hope so. I'm Detective Constable Bina Kaur, North Yorkshire Police. Can I come in, please? It's a matter of some urgency.'

A momentary pause. 'ID. I need to see ID. No ID. No entry. Council rules, I'm afraid. No exceptions. Sorry.'

'Will a warrant card do?'

'Yes.'

Bina thrust her warrant card towards the fish eye and the door's electromagnetic lock clicked and released. She gave a thumbs up, reached for the door handle.

'Wait in reception. I'll come down and sign you in,' a voice crackled from the intercom.

'Will do.'

Upstairs, hinges creaked, and a door slammed. A gangly, thin-faced man in his mid-thirties appeared at the top of the stairs. He bounded down. The man wore flared white jeans, a Space Invaders t-shirt and sneakers. He skidded to a halt on the timber parquet next to Bina. Reaching to his face, he pushed chrome effect John Lennon-style glasses along his nose.

'Hi, I'm Tim Warren. I work nights here. Official title is Senior CCTV Officer. I prefer Trainee Spook – it's cooler. Much cooler. What can I do for you?'

Bina gave him her best smile. 'Any chance I can view the CCTV recordings near Clifford's Tower for the early hours of this morning, please? Sorry, but I can't go into the whys and the wherefores. What I can say is... We're interested in the movements of one particular individual. Someone slipped through the net. With a helping hand from you guys, we'd like to get him back.'

Warren shrugged his shoulders. 'Cool. No worries. Ought not be too difficult. Good coverage there. Let's get you signed in. We'll take it from there. The council is a stickler for bureaucracy.'

* * *

An hour later, Bina said her goodbyes to Tim, stepped outside and called Wardell on her mobile. He answered on the first ring.

'How did you get on? You still at the control centre?'

'I am.'

'And did you see him?'

'Yes, I did.'

'And?'

'And I know how the sly sod slipped the leash. I also know where he went afterwards.'

'Excellent work, Bina. I'm all ears.'

'Sly bugger abseiled down the building facade. Seems he came prepared.'

'Where did he go from there?'

'We tracked him as far as Clifford Street. There, he turned right onto Coppergate, left onto Parliament Street. After that we lost him for a little while. When he reappeared, he was on Museum Street. To cut a long story short, boss, he returned to the hostel.'

'The hostel, eh?'

'Yes, boss. When I say hostel, I mean directly opposite.'

'Opposite? Why opposite? I'm not with you,' Wardell said.

'Colm approached and opened the driver's door of a white Ford Transit Connect parked opposite the hostel. He leaned in, pistol-whipped the middle-aged man sat in the driver's seat and dumped him unconscious in the back of the van.'

'And then?'

'And then, he got into the driver's seat and drove off.'

'Bloody hell, it never rains, but it pours. I expect you know what I'm going to say next?'

'Did I get the reg?'

'Correct. Well, did you?'

'Yes, boss, I did. Can you guess what it is, boss?'

'Don't mess about, Bina, it's too early for mind games. Is it the same van?'

'Yes, boss. It was CY12 OWN.'

40

FRIDAY 9TH JANUARY 2015, 8.30 A.M

The explosive snake hiss of air brakes releasing, and annoying tinny radio voices, woke the sleeping Colm. Coming to, he reached out, grasped the steering wheel and dragged up. As he did so, glimpsing movement in his peripheral vision, he looked to the door mirror and the reflected image of the Volvo truck. Inside the Volvo's cab, the driver pulled the curtains closed and the radio voices fell silent.

Flicking sleep from the corners of eyes, he gazed across the featureless battleship-grey sky past the windscreen. Given the paucity of daylight, unsure of the time, he exhaled a weary breath and looked to the dashboard clock. Half eight, yet it felt much earlier.

Reaching for the ignition, he spun the key and the diesel engine clattered to life. He sat and waited for the temperature needle to rise.

Behind him, the truck's cab curtains twitched. *Whatever*, thought Colm, *I was here first...*

Yawning, he spun gritty eyes to the passenger seat and the

Quality Street tin. Leaning left, he placed a flattened palm on the lid and felt the ice-cold desire for retribution settle his heart.

His gaze settled on the man, bound by heavy chains in the footwell, before returning to the road ahead.

41

FRIDAY 9TH JANUARY 2015, 4.30 P.M

Passing through open countryside into woodland, Colm's gaze settled on the narrow sliver of silvery asphalt receding in the rearview mirror. Satisfied no one was following, eyes straining against the gloom, he slowed the van and scanned the tree line for the boathouse entrance. Rounding a corner, the van's headlights picked out a hand painted sign nailed to a tree at a break in the trees. The sign read: 'PRIVATE – ASKRIGG BOAT CLUB – MEMBERS ONLY'.

Seeing the sign, a deluge of memories flooded into Colm's head: blazing summer days; boozy nights; friendships forged, and lost, and frantic drunken rolls in the hay behind the clubhouse.

Casting reminiscences into the long grass, he slowed the van at a break in the trees, spun the steering wheel left and turned off onto a gravel track. Passing along the track, the suspension wallowed, crashed and bottomed out and he slowed to a crawl. Fifty metres along, a pair of mysterious green eyes caught in the headlights and an owl scuttled past just inches past the windscreen. Crashing through a pothole, a muffled grunt echoed around the cabin. Negotiating through an arch of tall oaks, he skidded the van to a halt in the middle of the gravel car park.

Rolling out of the van, he rounded the bonnet and dragged the passenger door open. He stood, gathering his breath. Adrenaline coursed through his veins like liquid fire. Chilled air tickled his nostrils and ran to his lungs, but failed to extinguish the flames. Cocking his head on one side, listening hard, he heard wheezing, tortured breaths from the passenger side footwell. He looked off, focused distantly, looked back, saw him curled in footwell. Hunkering down, he reached in twisted the tie wraps securing the man's wrists and ankles. Reassured, with the end almost in sight, he allowed himself a smile. Balling his fists, he leaned in, placed extended arms under the man's armpits and took the weight. Lowering the bound man into the passenger seat, he reared from the cabin.

The bound man's nostrils flared. Glowering, he mumbled something unintelligible under the gag. Panicking, using his feet as a pivot against the floor, he bounced up and down. Half a minute later, his struggles ceased. Quietening, he groaned. Angry wild eyes settled on Colm denouncing his existence.

'Calm down. You're wasting your time,' Colm said, settling onto his haunches, bringing his gaze level with the bound man's. 'Unlike you, fella, I'm a pro, trained by the British Army – the best army in the world. I've completed tours in Iraq and Afghanistan. So shut up. Savvy up. And listen. I want information.'

Colm removed the man's gag. He sucked a long breath, exhaled. Colour returning to his face.

'I'll keep this simple. I know what you've done, who you've murdered. I want information. Don't even think about lying. It won't wash. Get what I want, you'll get to live. You keeping up?'

'Yes. What do you want to know? As if I can't guess.'

'Guess away.'

'You want to know who I'm working for? Where you can find them? You're planning on settling the score. Am I right?'

'Perceptive. Well done. A hundred percent right.'

'If I give you what you want, what do I get?'

Colm sniffed. Shrugged. 'You get to live.'

'I see. High stakes, then.'

'The highest.'

The man rattled the chains around his wrists and ankles. 'How do I know I can trust you?'

'Good question. I suppose that's for me to know...'

He finished Colm's sentence. 'And me to find out.'

'Correct.'

The bound man drew a long breath. Fell silent. Considered his predicament. Two long minutes passed.

'In the glove box, you'll find a mobile. The Irishman – my contact – he's listed in contacts under FROC. That's right, FROC. Weird, I know. He's expecting a text confirming the job's complete. There was going to be a handover.'

'A text confirming you've killed me and cut out my tongue, you mean? Like you did to the others? That kind of text?'

'I'm saying nothing.'

'Is that advisable?'

The man shrugged. 'Not really. All I know is he's gone to ground. He must've been getting twitchy, I suppose.'

Colm, forehead creasing, opened the glove box, reached in and took out a Samsung mobile.

'Password.'

'COSTA.'

Colm typed COSTA and the phone unlocked.

'Why FROC?'

'My hands are numb.'

Colm shook his head. 'All in good time. Why FROC?'

A resigned sigh. 'FROC. It's an abbreviation.'

'Go on.'

'Father O'Connell.'

'O'Connell! I should've known.'

'You know one another from way back, don't you?'

'Yes. Where is he?'

'God's honest truth... I don't know. I was supposed to text him, and he'd text back with a location. We'd meet, do the handover, job done.'

'When you had a full house?'

'What can I say?'

'Nothing. Tonight, it ends.'

Colm, straightening, closed the passenger side door and looked off into the distance. A minute passed. He marvelled at the stars. Spinning around, resolve burning in his gut, he strode over and dragged the passenger door open. A sulphurous mist of hate drifted behind his eyes. Reaching in, he placed the gag across the man's mouth.

'You reckon you're a hard man, don't you? Consider yourself the physical embodiment of evil. You don't know the meaning of the word. I do. I've seen and met evil. Fuck's sake, I *became* evil.' Closing his eyes, he drew air in through his nostrils. 'Listen to me, getting all het up about you... I mean, why should I? Enough of this bullshit!'

Colm dragged him from the car by the hair and launched him onto the wet gravel. He landed in a puddle with a splash.. Eyes ablaze, Colm leered over him, spittle drooling down his chin, sculptured muscles coiled.

'This first one is for Billy!'

Colm aimed his right boot at the man's ribcage beneath the armpits. Swung his leg from the hip with venom.

'Ugh!'

A sickening crack and the pneumatic release of air echoed into the darkness. The man curled into a ball.

Another kick.

'Ugh!'

Colm adjusted his position, took several steps back and a step to the left. Narrowing his eyes, he sought his target in the gloom. Found it. Raced forward. Launched a grievous kick at the curve of a jaw.

'This, you bastard, is for Jimmy!'

The nauseating snap of bone smashed to oblivion echoed from the trees.

'Argh!'

'This, motherfucker, is for Niall. God rest his soul.'

Colm took two long steps back, rocked on his heels, set his legs wide and found his balance. Stock still, he stalled, joined his fingers into a pyramid and sucked long breaths. Wiping his sweated brow, he relaxed his arms by his sides and looked up. Drawing breath, he raced forward and kicked the bound man in the head. The man's head settled onto his shoulder at an impossible angle. Blood – black under the moonlight – streamed from his ears, nose and mouth.

Silence.

'And this is for my beautiful son, dead inside that fucking tin.'

The last kick landed without response. Colm spat on the body lying face down in the mud. Two minutes later, lust satiated, he raced around to the driver's door, jumped in and started the engine. Cranking hard on the steering wheel, he aligned the front wheels with the unconscious man's head. Selecting first, he released the clutch. The van scrabbled on the loose gravel, lurched forward, and the long travel suspension passed noiselessly across the man's broken skull.

Colm jumped out of the van, raced back and heaved the lifeless body onto his shoulders in a fireman's lift. Staggering to the river, he dumped the body into the water, watched it disappear into the silt, turned and returned to the van.

42

High on adrenaline, Colm turned left out of the track and headed north. Keen to distance himself from the broken body lying at the bottom of the River Ouse, he pressed hard on the accelerator, and raced through the gears.

Five minutes and four miles later, rain speared against the windscreen from a moody sky and the tarmac took on a glossy sheen. To dispel the mist of condensation burgeoning from the bottom of the windscreen, he maxed the heater. As the condensation cleared, light-headed, he stepped off the accelerator too early at a sharp left-hander and the van slid uncontrollably across the wet tarmac. A stab of brakes brought the van under control.

Exhaling with relief, a metal tool box crashed against the mesh dividing the cabin from the load area at Colm's shoulder. He jumped. Nerves jangling, waves of tiredness roiling through, he tightened his grip on the steering wheel. With twenty-three hours without sleep taking its toll, he knew he should get some much-needed sleep.

Pulling in, he killed the engine and stabbed the interior light to life. Unbuckling from the seatbelt, he spun and collected of the

Quality Street tin, readying himself. Caressing cool metal, his hand faltered on the tin and a tragic hollowness overcame him. Removing his hand, he sat back and gazed out through the windscreen.

A tidal wave of grief consumed him and he cried. He cried for his murdered son inside the tin on the seat beside him, for Evelyn, and their lost life together, and Billy, Jimmy and Niall. Most of all, he cried for himself.

* * *

Ten minutes later, exhausted, he reached for the dead man's mobile, tabbed into and opened text messaging. He typed a terse message, selected the recipient, FROC.

```
job done
    text through location/postcode to meet
    cash on collection ... used notes
    best time 4 you?
    let me know...
```

He sent the message twice more. Satisfied, he cranked the seat into a horizontal position, lay back and closed his eyes.

Sleep took him within a minute.

43

FRIDAY 9TH JANUARY 2015, 5.10 P.M

History has a habit of repeating itself, thought Wardell. *Here I am, coastward bound on a murder case, with David Watts beside me.*

'You want a job doing, David, then you had better do it yourself,' Wardell said, with a sigh. 'My old man swore by it. And do you know something?'

'What boss?'

'The grumpy old bugger nailed it. Nobody ever said a truer word. I mean... How difficult can it be keeping tabs on a man locked inside a hotel room with only two exits? I ask you? It's hardly Houdini in the maze at bloody Hampton, is it?'

Watts cast a salutary glance at Wardell, shrugged. 'No, boss, it isn't. You'll want someone's neck on the block, I expect?'

'What would be the point? What good would it do?'

Static burst from the speakers. 'DI Wardell?' asked a familiar female voice. 'Over.'

Wardell cleared his throat with a cough. 'Speaking. Have you got anything for me? Over.'

'Alan, it's Jackie. There's been a positive sighting, albeit electronic, of the white van you're interested in.'

'Go on, Jackie.'

'Registration CY12 OWN triggered an ANPR camera five minutes ago on the A1235.'

Wardell interjected. 'Exactly where, Jackie? I need a precise location. Lives are at risk. Over.'

'Five miles south of Robin–' Whoops, pops and whistles, obliterated Jackie's voice.

'Control. Can you hear me?' Wardell asked. 'Speak up, Jackie. We're in and out of signal.'

The static faded. 'Reading you loud and clear, Alan. As I was saying... The target vehicle tripped ANPR five miles south of Robin Hood's Bay five minutes ago. Traffic is en route from Whitby as we speak. ETA ten. Repeat. Ten minutes. Over.'

'Thanks, Jackie. Tell Traffic to exercise caution. The driver's likely armed. He's ex-army with an axe to grind. Keep me appraised of any and everything, Jackie. Over.'

A bubble of anxiety burst inside Wardell's gut.

History *was* repeating itself.

'That was hard work. Head for the coast. Destination Robin Hood's Bay and don't you dare spare the horses,' Wardell said.

'Aye, aye, captain,' Watts replied, imitating Jack Sparrow. 'The coast it be.'

Wardell fell silent, massaged his chin. 'My money is on St Aubert's. Get on the blower to Charlie. Tell him to contact, Whitby and Scarborough. I want all the uniforms they can muster, and an armed response unit sent over to St Aubert's PDQ. Warn them about the possibility of him being armed.'

'Isn't that going overboard a bit, boss? He's only one man.'

'Walsh as the potential to be a one-man army. Best we treat him with the utmost respect. In fact, let's go one better. Contact Bina. Get her on the blower to air support in Wakefield. I want the helicopter up and tasked to locate that damned white van. It'll stick out like a sore thumb under the spotlight. Colm Walsh is a loose cannon. There's every chance he'll do something stupid.'

'You think so?'

'I do. Of course I hope I'm wrong, but I fear I'm not,' Wardell replied. 'Lead boots, David, lead boots...'

44

FRIDAY 9TH JANUARY 2015, 6.45 P.M

'Slow down, Tom. The roads around here are lethal,' Traffic Officer PC Ryan Lloyd said, as the wipers dumped the deluge of rain from the windscreen. 'There's a farm coming up. Most probably, cow shite all over the road. It'll be slippery as hell.'

PC Tom Sanderson nodded, stared at the road ahead. The Volvo Estate entered a sweeping, undulating right handed bend. Sanderson feathered the brakes and negotiated the corner.

'Keep your eyes peeled. We're looking for a white Transit Connect on an '08. Driver's a white Caucasian male,' Sanderson said. 'No passengers.'

'Got it.'

'He's likely armed. We're to exercise caution.'

A pair of headlights raced towards them, illuminating the tall pines bordering the road.

'Bloody idiot's got full beam on, I reckon,' Sanderson said, shielding his eyes with a raised hand. 'Ryan, when he goes past, have a gander at the reg. It could be our man.'

'Oscar Kilo.'

Twenty yards ahead, the headlights dimmed. A white box

raced past in a blur, exceeding the speed limit by some margin.

Lloyd spun and glimpsed o8 and the last three letters of the number plate: OWN.

'It's him! Positive ID on the reg. Spin round in the farm entrance. I'll radio it in.'

'You do that,' Sanderson said, switching on the siren and blues-and-twos. 'Add speeding to his charge sheet. Tosspot must've been doing almost a tonne.'

Lloyd collected the radio handset. 'Control. This is Echo Yankee Foxtrot four-five. The suspect vehicle has just passed our location travelling north on the A1230 towards Whitby. We're turning in pursuit. Request immediate assistance. Over.'

'Received and understood. Echo Yankee Foxtrot four-five. Help will be with you soon. Over.'

'Hold on tight, Ryan,' Sanderson boomed, doing a one-hundred eight degrees smoothly choreographed turn. Sanderson pressed hard on the accelerator and the Volvo sank onto its haunches and blasted forward. The turbo's waste gate burped like a morning-after drunk.

Half a mile ahead, crimson taillights glowed under braking and the van disappeared around a corner.

'Bugger's turned off towards Robin Hood's Bay,' Sanderson yelled. 'It's game on!'

Lloyd radioed it in. 'How far's the school?'

'Two miles. We ought to be able to catch up with him before he gets there. I know these roads like the back of my hand. I served my apprenticeship around here in my dad's old Mini Cooper. A right old go-kart it was. Stuck to the road like shit on a shovel, it did. Buckle up, Ryan. It's about to get hairy.'

'Take it easy, Tom. I'm on a promise on Friday.'

Tom Sanderson grinned, glowered demonically. 'O ye of little faith. Hold tight. You'll get your nookie, Friday. You're safe enough.'

Sanderson turned right into a narrow B-road signposted Robin Hood's Bay. The road just wide enough to accommodate two cars at a crawl. One hundred metres ahead, the van disappeared from sight over a blind brow.

'Hold on tight!' Sanderson bellowed

'Oh, shit!'

The Volvo arrived at the blind brow at eighty-five mph. Lloyd's fingers turned white on the door handle. Closing his eyes, gritting his teeth, the reptile side of his brain kicked in and he screamed, 'Whoa!'

As the powerful Volvo achieved positive lift, it won the battle with gravity, took off and speared through the air.

'What the flying fuck!' Lloyd screamed as the car's trajectory flattened.

'Whoa!' Sanderson yelled, relishing the moment.

'Brake!' Lloyd screamed. 'Van!'

'I've seen it.'

Fifty metres ahead, a white van stood stationary across the width of the road with the driver's door open. Light spilled out from the interior across the wet tarmac. Headlight beams speared the pines. The Volvo crash landed twenty metres from the van.

'Brace yourself,' Sanderson spat, dragging hard left on the steering wheel and pulling on the handbrake.

Skidding, engine wailing, the rear end danced out, and the Volvo slid sideways. Lloyd watched the flank of the van grow until it filled his field of vision. Casting his legs deep into the footwell, he braced himself for impact.

Sideways on, the Volvo slid to a halt two metres from, and parallel with the white van. Sanderson killed the engine. Silence enveloped the cabin but for the cooling clicks of the engine. Lloyd turned to Sanderson, laughed. 'Well done. That was bloody close.'

Sanderson, chest heaving with relief, a sheen of perspiration across his forehead, heaved a sigh. A thin smile arrived on his lips. He turned to Lloyd, said, 'You're welcome.'

The tapping sound of metal meeting glass resonated inside the cabin. Sanderson looked across. 'Don't look now, Ryan, only...'

'What now, for fuck's sake?'

'Only, someone's pointing a gun at you.'

* * *

Within five minutes, Colm had handcuffed both officers to a gate. Stepping away, he engaged the safety and slipped the pistol into the holster hung under his right arm.

'It's been lovely meeting you, guys. I only wish I could stay and chat, but there's important business to attend to,' Colm said, grinning. 'Goodbye.'

As Colm stepped away, a mobile beeped. Colm recovered the mobile from an inside pocket. A text message displayed on the screen of the dead man's mobile:

St Aubert's Boarding School, Robin Hood's Bay.
YO23 2CV
    Gatehouse Cottage,
    50 yards from main entrance. COME ASAP.

Beaming, Colm penned a reply from the dead man.

be there in ten... leave front and back doors
unlocked... lights on...

45

FRIDAY 9TH JANUARY 2015, 7.00 P.M

Colm negotiated the nose of the white van through the narrow stone pillars at the entrance to St Aubert's, geared down, and sped up. The engine bellowed, tyres yelped, and the van darted forward.

Fifty yards ahead on the left, half hidden in the trees, lights burned inside a stone chalet style bungalow.

Colm imagined O'Connell as the spider at the centre of the web, poised to rush toward the chalet door, pay the hitman and collect the spoils.

Inside Colm's head, the years dissolved and St Aubert's became real again. Colm's gaze settled on the school. Nothing seemed to have changed. Seeing it, a maelstrom of confusion, bitterness, heartbreak and fear ran through him. He saw the boy. Remembered the restless, broken soul, unsure of his place in the world. The pain, renewed and alive, felt almost touchable. His fractured heart fuelled by despair, anger and hate.

Be quick. Get inside. Say your piece. Finish it. Then disappear on the wind. He told himself.

Cognisant of the futility of anger unless harnessed and channelled, he drew a long, calming breath. If the army had taught him anything, it was that.

Killing the engine, he stepped out and raced to the chalet's front door and placed the battered Quality Street down on the step. Reaching up, he removed the pistol from the holster, released the empty clip and slid in six bullets.

Left ear placed against the door, he drew a breath. Inside, the silence was absolute. He looked to the tin. Somewhere distant, a siren whirled. A police car? Ambulance? Fire engine? It was impossible to tell. The distant whoop-whoop of a helicopter getting louder. His sudden realisation that the apparatus of the law, intent on denying him justice, was racing toward him.

Stay calm.

Speed up.

Get this done.

Colm opened the door, paused on the threshold and peered inside. Once his eyes had adjusted to the gloom, he gazed along a narrow hallway ending in a panelled door.

Beyond the panelled door, he heard the shuffle of feet over timber. The door creaked open and a stooped figure appeared in the opening. He recognised O'Connell the instant he laid eyes on him.

'Boss, Jackie in control can't get raise traffic. Officers Lloyd and Sanderson aren't responding. She's worried,' Watts said.

Wardell exhaled a resigned sigh. 'Walsh? I hope he's not done nothing stupid?'

More than probable, thought Watts. 'Traffic had visual on the van heading towards Robin Hood's Bay, then nothing. It's worrying,' he said.

The radio hissed and a monotone male voice cut through the

static. 'This is police helicopter Bravo Charlie Echo four-five. Advise traffic Echo Yankee Foxtrot four-five is stationary on the B2345 half a mile from the junction with A1230. We have visual on two officers. Handcuffed. Repeat. Handcuffed to a gate. Urgent assistance requested. Anticipated overhead the school in two, repeat, two minutes. Over.'

Wardell and Watts's eyes darted to the satnav. Adhering to speed limits, St Aubert's was still fifteen miles away. Wardell looked to Watts.

'Give it the beans, David. Permission granted to break the speed limit by a big margin.'

Watts grinned. 'Challenge accepted.'

'Damn. I thought you'd say,' Wardell said, hunkering down, grasping the door handle. 'Safety fast, David, safety fast.'

46

THURSDAY 11TH SEPTEMBER 1975, 1.00 A.M

Lemon disinfectant and the iron smell of blood hung thick in the air. A draught of icy air blasted in through the open window and rattled the curtains on the rail. The pages of a prayer book fluttered on the desk. Bloodied cotton sheets piled high in wicker baskets. Father Brian Murphy's lifeless corpse lay wrapped in plastic sheeting on the landing – a human-sized chrysalis of broken flesh and bone. Blood speckled with grey brain matter pooled around his head.

'That'll do for now,' Stan said, gathering breath. 'I'll see to the mattress tomorrow. Take it to the tip. We're done for now.'

O'Connell straining upright, vertebrae clicking, lifted the table lamp and cast light around the bedroom. He nodded solemnly. 'Our business here is complete. I'll have the sisters give it the once over, tomorrow morning,' he said, glancing over a shoulder to the landing. 'All we need to do now – you, me and Colm – is get him buried whilst it's still dark.'

Stan studied the priest with ill-concealed bewilderment. 'I'm not sure that's such a good idea, Father. The boy's traumatised enough.'

'You think so?'

'I do.'

O'Connell's rolled his eyes to the ceiling and exhaled an exasperated sigh. 'That boy just killed a man. He must never forget that. Enough of this nonsense,' O'Connell said, stepping onto the landing, sinking to his knees and grabbing the corpse by the ankles through the plastic sheeting. O'Connell glowered at Stan. 'Are you just going to stand there watching me struggle? I want this done and dusted. Six feet under is the best place for him now. God rest his soul.'

Stan wiped his brow, shook his head, stepped forward. 'Aye, I expect you're right. You take the feet. I'll take the head.'

They settled Murphy's lifeless, cocooned body into a wheeled laundry bin. O'Connell closed the lid. They wheeled the bin to the front door and set it against the wall.

'Leave it here. Follow me,' O'Connell said, setting off to the chapel.

Sister Mary O'Toole sat on a low stool outside the sacristy door, head down, reading. Hearing their approach, looking up, she closed the Bible and settled it onto her lap.

'Has he said anything?' O'Connell asked. 'Or tried to escape?'

A brief shrug. 'There's been an occasional whimper, yes, Father. He's not moved an inch.'

'Good. I'll take over. Go upstairs and do your best to settle the boys down. I heard voices, floorboards creaking.'

Sister O'Toole clutched the Bible to her chest, rose, and scurried away.

'Father!'

O'Connell, feeling a firm hand settle on his shoulder, swung to face Stan.

'What now?' O'Connell barked. 'Take your hand off me.'

Stan released his grip. 'Father, it's best that I talk to him alone.'

'You?'

'Yes, me. He listens to me. We connect with one another.'

O'Connell's eyes narrowed, nose wrinkled. He fell silent. When he spoke again it was in a low, measured, voice. 'What do you plan to say?'

'What you tell me to. The cottage, Father, I want the cottage. Tell me what to say. I'm not very good with words.'

O'Connell grinned, revealed nicotine-stained teeth between grey lips. 'Tell him he must never discuss with another living soul, his time at St Aubert's. He should tell no one about either, the baby, or the events of tonight. Tell him what's done's done. It's best all round that he makes a fresh start. Tell him God forgives him. That God forgives us all. Colm must know, by the grace of God and the power vested in me by the Church, that I've granted him absolution from his sins. By that same power, tell him I won't inform the police, on condition of his silence. That, Stan, is what I want you to tell him. Will you do it? Will you persuade him to accept this bargain, not only for me, but for Father Brian, you, and himself. Can you do that, Stan?'

Stan ran a hand over his chin, stress etched in the lines across his forehead and around his mouth. A long half minute passed.

'I will so long as I get my cottage.'

Stan thrust out a hand. They shook hands.

'I'm a man of my word. A man of God. Persuade Colm to keep his counsel, to accept our bargain, do that, and the cottage is yours.'

'Don't worry, I will. I'll get you your bargain, Father.'

47

THURSDAY 8TH JANUARY 2015, 7.15 P.M

Colm held the pistol in his right hand; the battered Quality Street tin tucked under his left armpit.

From the end of the hallway, O'Connell's hollow gaze settled on Colm and the dark eye of instant death. Resigned to his fate, his shoulders drooped. His gaze met Colm's. 'I see you've got the tin. So much for the plan... It was inevitable something would go wrong...'

'As luck would have it, yes,' Colm said, raising the pistol, aligning the sights with O'Connell's chest. 'Do you recognise me, yet?'

'I do. How could I forget? You've not changed. The years have been kind to you. Of late, I've been giving the subject of *you* a lot of thought.'

'You have?'

'I have. Can I take the weight off my feet? My legs, as you might imagine, they're not what they once were.'

'Is the lounge through there?' Colm nodded left.

'It is. There's a fire, lamp, bookcase and a two comfy armchairs. What more does an old man need?'

'Not much more, I suppose. This place, O'Connell,' Colm asked, 'is it yours?'

'It's my special place, yes. When first I retired, I used to come here most weekends. I love this place. Don't ask me why, but it's got the feel of Killarney about it. We holidayed there every year when I was a boy. Nowadays, I don't come here as often as I'd like. Can I offer you a word of advice, Colm?'

Colm frowned. 'If you must.'

'Don't get old. I can't say as I recommend it. Can I take the weight off?'

'I'll try to remember your wise words when I'm old and grey. Take it slow, Father. We'll talk in the lounge.'

'Talk. Now isn't that a fine idea. Talking helps.'

O'Connell shuffled along the hallway, stepped right through an arched opening. Colm followed, kept a safe distance between them.

The elderly priest lowered into a threadbare, paisley print armchair positioned under the window. Two identical armchairs sat opposite one another across a mahogany coffee table. An art deco style ceramic tiled fireplace central between the armchairs. An ancient electric bar fire gave the room a warm orange glow. O'Connell reached over his shoulder and switched on a tall lamp. The room smelt of damp, tobacco, and furniture polish.

Colm, lowering into the armchair opposite O'Connell, settled the pistol along his thigh, angled it so the barrel pointed at O'Connell's chest. He placed the Quality Street tin on the coffee table. Only three feet separated them.

They sat, not speaking. Two minutes passed. The only sound the distant whoop of sirens.

Colm spoke first. 'I'm flattered.'

'Might I ask why?'

'*You*, giving *me* a lot of thought. In a weird way, it's flattering.'

O'Connell leaned forward, stabbed a crooked finger at Colm. 'You were always different from the others.'

'I'm not with you?'

'You were the spirited one. The one to put up a fight. I knew you'd be the one to make something of yourself. I've followed your progress with interest.'

'You have?'

'Yes, I have. You became a captain in the British Army and were awarded the Distinguished Service Medal. That's quite an achievement. You should be proud of yourself.'

'You've done your research.'

'I have. There's an old saying... Know thy self, know thy enemy, a thousand battles, a thousand victories.'

'I'm familiar with it,' Colm said.

O'Connell chuckled, sniffled, and wiped a bulb of snot with the sleeve of his wool cardigan. 'I'm the one that's lost the most important battle.'

'You have?'

'I have. Isn't it obvious? I'm the one that's staring down the business end of a gun. It's not how I imagined it would end.'

'That's not what I'm referring to O'Connell.'

'You've lost me. Explain yourself. Age, it addles the brain.'

'Why did you renege on our *understanding*? Our bargain? It's obvious, you and your cronies went back on it. Why stir things up? What we agreed – you, me and Stan. All these years, it's protected us. That night, Murphy deserved to die. *You*, deserved to die. In the immediate aftermath, Stan talked me out of killing you. He brought me to my senses. Something – I'm not sure what – changed. What changed, O'Connell? Why the sudden need for murder? Why the desire to erase the past?'

O'Connell ran a wrinkled hand over his chin, averted his gaze to the bookshelf and studied the spines.

'Well?' Colm bellowed. 'I haven't got all night. What the fuck changed? I need to know. My friends, O'Connell, under your direction, are dead. I was next. That isn't a nice thought.'

O'Connell's yellowing eyes drifted from the bookcase and met Colm's. 'Organisations changed, Colm. Fresh blood came in. The new people became empowered. They flexed their muscles. Powerful people can only take so much, you see. One damaging scandal after another. Most of them, I hasten to add, malicious without a shred of evidence. Something positive needed doing. They hatched a plot. Don't press me for details, because I don't have any. Someone high up changed tack and went on the offensive. They dragged skeletons out of cupboards and buried them. I thought it the wrong strategy. St Aubert's was unnecessary. Time had passed. The hurt had become bearable, but it was out of my hands. Those that decide these things, they're all powerful. I told them about our understanding. I gave them a potted history. They wouldn't listen. I wasted my breath. They'd already made up their minds. The rest, as they say, is history.'

The helicopter overhead rattled roof slates. Window panes shook. Voices were close outside. Radio chatter. Spiralling blue light.

'Shit! Old Bill,' Colm hissed. 'I want you to reach behind you and close the curtains. Do it nice and slow. No sudden movements.'

'And why, would I do that?'

Anger flared in Colm's eyes. 'Just do it. You're not in a position to bargain. Your bargaining days, O'Connell, are over.'

'And what if I don't? Will it make any difference? Given the police are braying at the door, you're going to kill me, anyway. You want justice. Get it over with. Shoot me. Put me out of my misery. Do it while you've got the chance. This time – since there's no one to talk you out of it – don't fluff your lines. All I'd ask is you make it quick.'

Colm, steadying the pistol, sighted the barrel on O'Connell's forehead. Rising, he inched over and closed the curtains. Rounding the armchair, he clipped O'Connell on the side of the head with the gun.

'Ow! That hurt.'

'Shut it. Manipulative bastard. Next time, do as you're told. I don't what to hear any more of your psychobabble. Alright?'

'Alright...'

Colm glowered, pondered his predicament. Killing a defenceless old man in cold blood would mean only one thing – they'd throw away the key. Release O'Connell, and justice would be denied. In battle, he'd killed many men, but never cold blood. It just didn't sit right.

'Let me get this right. What you're saying is... They murdered Billy, Jimmy and Niall to satisfy the whims of *fresh blood*?'

O'Connell dipped his head. 'Yes. New people bring new ideas. They get their way. They become too powerful. And, as everyone with a breath of air in their lungs knows, power corrupts. Power sullies thinking. Things happen... unnecessary things. There are consequences and the world spins on a different axis.' O'Connell glanced to the battered Quality Street tin. 'For what it's worth Colm, I'm sorry about that. It was none of my doing. Murphy was a loose cannon. He acted without my approval or knowledge. He performed the abortion. It was his decision. I knew nothing about it until it was too late.'

'You're a saint. *That*, has a *fucking* name.'

'I'm sorry. I never knew. Who christened him? Murphy?'

'No. Evelyn christened him. She gave our boy a name as he lay dead in her arms, just before Murphy took him away. She called him Thomas. Tommy.'

'I see. That's a good name. A strong name.'

'Christ, listen to you. Sanctimonious old bastard, that you are. You've not changed. Look at you, sitting there, making remarks, acting like the abuse never happened, when we both know you don't have a shred of decency in your entire body. You terrorised us. Inflicted so much pain. You concealed murder, yet you have the gall to sit there – all superior. *Being* superior. Behaving like you've done nothing wrong. You make me want to puke, O'Connell. You're the devil incarnate. It's over for you, O'Connell. There's no bargain to protect you anymore.'

'COLM WALSH, WE KNOW YOU'RE IN THERE. WE KNOW YOU'RE ARMED. NOBODY NEEDS TO GET HURT. COME OUT SLOWLY, WITH YOUR HANDS ABOVE YOUR HEAD. PUT THE GUN ON THE GROUND.' Wardell's amplified voice boomed through the night.

'The Cavalry, O'Connell, have arrived too late,' Colm sneered.

He tensioned the index finger of his right hand on the trigger. 'Anything you want to confess, O'Connell, before you go to hell? This is your last chance to repent your sins.'

O'Connell shrugged. The light from the hallway dimmed. O'Connell's gaze shifted right toward the archway into the hallway. Stan Oldroyd stood in the opening clutching a shotgun. Colm followed O'Connell's gaze.

O'Connell returned his gaze to Colm with a look of weary resignation. 'I've nothing more to say. I've said all I'm ever going to say. Talk, now, would be pointless. My soul, like Murphy's and the nuns that served us, is beyond absolution.'

BOOM! BOOM!

Two gunshots rang out. Blasts of supercharged air ran past Colm's face. Fierce heat licked his skin. O'Connell's head exploded in a fog of bloodied brains and shattered bone. The headless body keeled over, slid and settled on the arm of the chair. Bloody bubbles inflated and popped from O'Connell's severed oesophagus.

Stan stepped into the lounge.

Colm bolted up. 'Stan!'

'Hey up, lad, long time, no see. Sorry to gatecrash, only, I was out and about checking the pheasants around the back when I heard all the commotion. I came in the back door. I've been in the hall, listening. Some folk would say I was trespassing on private property. To be honest, lad, I'm past caring. I hope you don't mind me stealing thy thunder?' Stan nodded towards O'Connell's shattered body. 'Anyway, owner's not likely to sue, now, is he?'

'Hardly, Stan, hardly... Why did you fucking shoot him? Bastard was mine.'

'Calm darn, lad. And moderate thy language. There's no cause to use foul language.'

'Why, Stan? Why?'

'The truth, lad, that's why. I've done what's right. After you'd killed Murphy, I cut a deal with O'Connell. He agreed to transfer ownership of the cottage to me, in exchange for your silence about the abuse and their silence about you killing Murphy. It was the price they paid for *my* silence. The price they paid for *your* silence. Cast your mind back, lad. It was me who persuaded you to sweep it all under the carpet. I did a deal with the devil for my cottage. Don't for one minute think I'm proud of what I did, because I'm not. I've lived with the shame of that night ever since. I am ashamed. That bastard, the one over there with his head plastered all over the wall, he got what was he deserved. As for you... You need to collect your things, take the tin, your boy, and get off. Escape through the woods. It won't be long as it's crawling with police. Go now, while you can.'

'But...'

Stan interrupted Colm with a raised palm. 'But nothing! I'm not arguing with thee, lad. What's done's done. It's over with. I did what I ought've done years back. It's me that killed O'Connell. It's me they'll arrest, not you. I'm at the end of my life, you've got a lot of living to do. Now, I don't want to hear another squeak from thee. Go, while there's still time. Don't test me, lad, or I might change my mind and pass thee a smoking gun.'

Colm stood inches from his old friend. Their eyes met. Tears cascaded down Stan's cheeks and he pulled Colm into an embrace and hugged him, whispered in his ear, 'I'm truly, truly, sorry, lad. It should never to have got to this. Find Evelyn and give your boy a proper, Christian burial. Do it together. Give her my regards. Evelyn was a lovely lass.'

Pushing Colm away, Stan nodded towards the back door. Colm reached to the coffee table and picked up the Quality Street tin.

'I will, Stan, I promise... I will. I'll never forget what you've done here tonight. *Never*. You have my word.'

'That's enough for me. Now, *go!*'

Colm raced to the back door, opened it and peered outside into the darkness. Satisfied, he turned and waved goodbye.

'Go!' Stan boomed. 'And never look back...'

He watched Colm disappear into the woods. Smiling, he closed the door, threw the deadlock, settled his back against the door and slid to the floor.

Wiping tears from his cheeks, Stan chuckled, spun the shotgun around and placed the tip of the barrel in his mouth.

Drawing a long last breath, he pulled the trigger.

THANK YOU!

I hope you enjoyed reading **BEYOND ABSOLUTION** as much as I enjoyed writing it. If you did, I would be forever grateful if you could take a moment to leave a review on your preferred platform.

Reviews help others find my books and help me keep writing. I love hearing from readers. You can contact me via my facebook page, K W Cosgrave Author, or via my website. Here's the link to my WEBSITE.

www.indiumbooks.com

As a **THANK YOU,** I would like to offer you a **FREE SHORT STORY - MURDER AT DEVIL'S BRIDGE** when you sign up to my **PRIVILEGE CLUB**. All you have to do is follow this link and instructions. It's **FREE** to join and you can leave at any time.

www.indiumbooks.com

HAPPY READING!

ABOUT THE AUTHOR

Keiron Cosgrave has written four crime novels and one novella. He has also co-written two further crime novels with his partner in crime and life, Christine Hancock.

This is Keiron's second novel under the Indium Books imprint.

Keiron lives in Yorkshire with partner Christine and has two grown up sons, Oliver & Louis. Keiron loves writing, reading, scooters and fair weather fishing.

ALSO BY KEIRON COSGRAVE

NOVELS

Promises, Promises

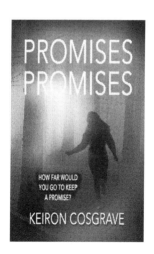

How far would you go to keep a promise?

After Kate and best friend Rose take revenge on their abuser at boarding school, their lives become macabrely connected forever. Years later, Kate's father reveals decades old secrets. The veneer of middle-class respectability fractures. A childhood promise is stretched to breaking. A family implodes.

When Kate's father is found murdered, DI Alan Wardell unravels a complex web of desire, betrayal and greed. More family members are murdered...

Will Wardell catch the brutal serial killer before Kate becomes his next victim?

A roller coaster ride of raw emotion, which builds towards a breath-taking climax.

With Menaces

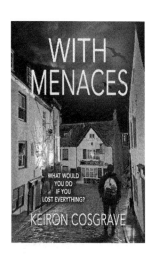

What would you do if you lost everything?

Cast on the scrap heap by his employers, pitied and despised by his soon-to-be ex-wife, Gavin Clark starts to lose his mind. Homeless and hungry, Gavin gets caught up in the seedy underworld of a bleak seaside town at the end of the line.

As he descends in the abyss, Gavin hatches a sinister scheme to heap revenge on those he believes have wronged him.

He becomes a vigilante on the wrong side of the law.

Can Wardell untangle the dark psychology and motives of a vengeful and elusive serial killer, before more lives are destroyed?

A powerful story of hate, anger and revenge...

The Celtic Cross Killer

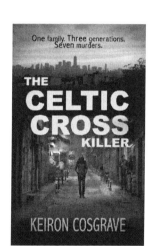

One family. Three generations.
Seven murders.

It is January 2005. New York is blanketed by snow. A killer driven by hatred roams the streets of Brooklyn.

Brooklyn pizzeria owner Ernest Costa leads a normal life. His business is thriving. He has a beautiful wife, and everything to live for. Returning home from work one freezing night, his life is snuffed out by a brutal and frenzied knife attack in a dark alley. His throat is slashed. A Celtic cross is slit deep across his back. Is the cross the signature of a psychopath? A recidivist who will strike again? Or is it an isolated attack? Someone knows the killer's identity...

Two years pass. The murder investigation stalls. Fingers are pointed at the senior detectives leading the manhunt. Removed from the case by his superiors, disgruntled NYPD Detective Antonio Pecarro decides to leave the force he once loved. He resigns and sets up as a private investigator.

Another body defiled with the same signature is discovered within sight of the victim's home. The victim's wife witnesses the killer leaving the scene. The killer's modus operandi is identical. Both victims are of Italian American heritage, of similar age and social standing. Is there a deranged serial killer driven by a compulsion to kill and bad blood walking the streets? Someone who will stop killing only when they are captured?

The investigation is re-launched. Criminal Psychologist Gerard Tooley is brought in. Progress is anaemic. Tensions bubble. Tooley is 'cut-free' from the team to pursue his own lines of investigation. Progress is made...

The heartbroken wife of the second victim decides to take matters into her own hands. She commissions P.I. Antonio Pecarro to identify and apprehend her husband's killer.

Another murder striking at the heart of the NYPD happens... Will Pecarro solve the riddle before the NYPD and catch the serial killer before he strikes again?

The Celtic Cross Killer is a complex fast-paced historical crime thriller with a twist that will keep the reader guessing until its breath-taking climax.

NOVELLA

Murder At Devil's Bridge

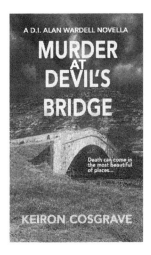

Death can come in the most beautiful of places...

When adulteress Claire Tomlinson is found murdered at a local beauty spot, suspicion falls upon her husband, Drew, and her lover, Owen.

But things aren't quite that simple.

Both men deny involvement in the killing and profess their innocence...

Can Detective Inspector Alan Wardell unravel this complex tale of lust, anger and revenge?

Not Mine To Take

What if your hopes and dreams become your worst nightmare?

When bestselling novelist Erin Moran discovers her husband's infidelity, the threads holding together her life, ten-year marriage and career, start to unravel.

Under pressure from her agent and best friend, Olivia Pope, to rewrite her rejected latest novel, Erin seeks sanctuary on Scalaig – an idyllic tidal island on the west coast of Scotland.

Broken and depressed, with only her faithful golden retriever Bella for company, Erin settles in for a summer of renewal at her beloved Scalaig Lodge. What starts out as an escape soon becomes something far more sinister.

The locals in the nearby town of Scaloon, seem resentful of her presence, and Erin can't understand why?

Alone and isolated, cut off from the mainland twice a day, Erin's imagination runs wild.

Are the rumours of kidnap and murder the stuff of legend perpetuated to scare away strangers and interlopers? Or is Erin being warned off?

After a series of unexplained events, Erin questions her sanity...

Is someone out there? Is someone watching her every move? Is someone biding their time?

Not Hers To Take

All lives are precious. Are some lives more precious than others?

Ruby Harper is lost...

Betrayed by the man she loves, ostracised by her wealthy mother and high-flying sister, Ruby runs away to a world populated by drug users and abusive men.

When her mother dies prematurely, Ruby finds the strength to rebuild her shattered life and start anew.

But life is never that simple... Ruby has something precious... Something people want...

Who can she trust?

Her sister? Her best friend? Her lover?

Who stands to gain the most from Ruby's death?

For more information, visit our website:

www.indiumbooks.com

Or my Facebook author page - K W Cosgrave Author

Printed in Great Britain
by Amazon